About the Author

ROBERT VAN GULIK was born in the Netherlands in 1910. He was educated at the Universities of Leyden and Utrecht, and served in the Dutch
diplomatic service in China and Japan for many years. His interest in
Asian languages and art led him to the discovery of Chinese detective
novels, and to the historical character of Judge Dee, famous in ancient
Chinese annals as a scholar-magistrate. Van Gulik subsequently began
writing the Judge Dee series of novels that have so captivated mystery
readers ever since. He died of cancer in 1967.

*The
Chinese
Nail
Murders*

Also by Robert Van Gulik

The Chinese Bell Murders

The Chinese Gold Murders

The Chinese Lake Murders

Judge Dee

The
Chinese
Nail
Murders

A Judge Dee
Detective Story

Robert Van Gulik

with nine plates drawn by the
author in Chinese style

HARPER

NEW YORK . LONDON . TORONTO . SYDNEY

HARPER

A hardcover edition of this book was published in 1961 by Harper & Row.

THE CHINESE NAIL MURDERS. Copyright © 1961 by Robert Van Gulik. All rights reserved. Printed in the United States of America. No part of this book may be used or reproduced in any manner whatsoever without written permission except in the case of brief quotations embodied in critical articles and reviews. For information, address HarperCollins Publishers, 195 Broadway, New York, NY 10007.

HarperCollins books may be purchased for educational, business, or sales promotional use. For information, please e-mail the Special Markets Department at SPsales@harper-collins.com.

First Perennial edition published 2005.

Library of Congress Cataloging-in-Publication Data

Gulik, Robert Hans Van, 1910–1967.
   The Chinese Nail Murders : a Judge Dee detective story / by Robert Van Gulik.—1st Perennial ed.
     p. cm.
"With nine plates drawn by the author in Chinese style."
ISBN 0-06-075139-8
   1. Di, Renjie, 629–700—Fiction. 2. Chin—History—Tang dynasty, 618–907—Fiction. 3. Judges—Fiction. I. Title

PR9130.9.G8C545 2005
823'.914—dc22   2004058747

     16 17 18 19 20   RRD(H) 11

Preface

The Chinese Nail Murders is the concluding novel of my series "Judge Dee Mysteries."

The present novel tells how the master detective of ancient China solved three crimes, a few months after he had been appointed magistrate of Pei-chow, a distant frontier district in the barren north of the Chinese Empire. A sketch map of the town is given on the endpapers, and in the Postscript will be found a list of Chinese sources, together with some general remarks on "Judge Dee Mysteries" and how and why they were written.

The novels of this series cover only the earlier half of Judge Dee's career, when he was serving as magistrate in various districts in the provinces. About this phase the Chinese historical records have little to say beyond the fact that he solved a great number of mysterious crimes. Concerning Judge Dee's career at court, however, those records go into considerable detail, for then the judge became a figure of national importance. He was one of the very few statesmen who could bring some influence to bear on Empress Wu, the cruel and dissolute but extremely capable woman who for fifty years ruled the T'ang Empire with an iron hand.[*] How Judge Dee tried to reform a corrupt administration and, falsely accused, was sentenced to be tortured to death; by what stratagem he succeeded in escaping from prison and how he effected his return to power; how thereafter he prevented the Empress from committing many a cruel deed and how, as crowning achievement of his career, he thwarted her scheme to place an unrightful heir on the Dragon Throne—all this proves clearly that fact is indeed stranger than fiction.

Judge Dee died in A.D. 700, seventy years old, after having occupied with distinction the highest civil and military posts in the Empire. He was survived by two sons, each of whom had a moderately successful official career. The historical records state, however, that Judge Dee's grandson, Dee Djien-mo, who died as Metropolitan Governor, again possessed the mellow wisdom and deep humanity of his famous grandfather.

During the ensuing centuries the Dee family from T'ai-yuan did not become prominent again in national affairs, although it did produce a few scholars and poets. The family still exists today. In 1936 I met in Shanghai one of Judge Dee's descendants, an amiable elderly gentleman who enjoyed some reputation as a connoisseur of antique paintings. But our conversation was limited to the exchange of the usual courtesies, for I could not then have foreseen that fourteen years later I would start to write several novels about his illustrious ancestor.

ROBERT VAN GULIK

* The second part of Judge Dee's career has been vividly described by Lin Yutang in his recent historical novel, *Lady Wu, a True Story* (W. Heinemann Ltd., London 1959, Chapter 37); there his name is transcribed Di Renjiay.

Contents

First Chapter: AN UNEXPECTED MEETING IN A GARDEN PA-
VILION; A FIENDISH MURDER IS REPORTED TO JUDGE DEE   1

Second Chapter: A PAPER MERCHANT ACCUSES AN ANTIQUE
DEALER; JUDGE DEE PROCEEDS TO THE SCENE OF THE
CRIME   12

Third Chapter: AN AUTOPSY IS CONDUCTED ON A HEADLESS
CORPSE; THE JUDGE CONSULTS WITH HIS FOUR LIEUTEN-
ANTS   27

Fourth Chapter: JUDGE DEE GOES OUT TO JOIN A HUNTING
DINNER; A SUSPECT IS ARRESTED BY THE MILITARY PO-
LICE   34

Fifth Chapter: TAO GAN TELLS ABOUT A CHAMPION'S
HOBBY; A CURIO DEALER IS HEARD IN THE TRIBUNAL   43

Sixth Chapter: TAO GAN GATHERS SOME CURIOUS INFORMA-
TION; HE GETS A GRATIS MEAL FROM A RICE MERCHANT   53

Seventh Chapter: TWO FRIENDS VISIT THE BOXER'S HOUSE; A ONE-EYED SOLDIER TELLS A SAD STORY   61

Eighth Chapter: JUDGE DEE SUMS UP TWO DIFFICULT CASES; A YOUNG MAN CONFESSES HIS MORAL MISTAKE   74

Ninth Chapter: JUDGE DEE TAKES HOME A LOST SMALL GIRL; HE HEARS THE NEWS ABOUT ANOTHER MURDER   84

Tenth Chapter: THE JUDGE INVESTIGATES A COWARDLY CRIME; HE FINDS A POISONED FLOWER IN A TEACUP   92

Eleventh Chapter: A CRUEL MURDER IS DISCUSSED IN THE TRIBUNAL; THE CORONER REPORTS ON A SUSPICIOUS OLD CASE   100

Twelfth Chapter: JUDGE DEE GOES TO VISIT MEDICINE HILL; A WOMAN DEFIES THE ORDERS OF THE TRIBUNAL   112

Thirteenth Chapter: THE JUDGE CONVERSES WITH AN ANTIQUE DEALER; HE IS TOLD THE EFFECT OF LACQUER POISONING   119

Fourteenth Chapter: A YOUNG WIDOW IS HEARD IN THE TRIBUNAL; SHE IS PUNISHED FOR CONTEMPT OF COURT   129

Fifteenth Chapter: SERGEANT HOONG VISITS THE COVERED MARKET; HE MEETS THE HOODED MAN IN A WINE HOUSE   134

Sixteenth Chapter: THREE HORSEMEN RETURN FROM AN EARLY RIDE; A MISGUIDED WOMAN TELLS ABOUT HER FOLLY   141

Seventeenth Chapter: JUDGE DEE EXPLAINS A FIENDISH MURDER; HE LEARNS THE SECRET OF THE PAPER CAT   151

Eighteenth Chapter: THE CORONER'S WIFE REPORTS ON TWO PRISONERS; A YOUNG WIDOW IS AGAIN HEARD IN THE TRIBUNAL   162

Nineteenth Chapter: A MALICIOUS WOMAN REVILES THE MAGISTRATE; THE SUDDEN TRANSFORMATION OF A PAPER CAT   168

Twentieth Chapter: AN AUTOPSY IS CONDUCTED IN THE CEMETERY; A VERY SICK MAN TELLS A STRANGE STORY   176

Twenty-first Chapter: A CAPTAIN ARRIVES WITH AN URGENT LETTER; THE JUDGE REPORTS IN THE ANCESTRAL HALL   185

Twenty-second Chapter: JUDGE DEE RECEIVES AN UNEXPECTED VISIT; HE DECIDES TO CONDUCT A SECOND AUTOPSY   191

Twenty-third Chapter: THE TRIBUNAL PREPARES A SPECIAL SESSION; A WOMAN TELLS AT LAST HER AMAZING TALE   196

Twenty-fourth Chapter: THE JUDGE GOES OUT ON A SECRET EXCURSION; HE PAYS A SECOND VISIT TO MEDICINE HILL   203

Twenty-fifth Chapter: THE CORONER PROFFERS A STARTLING ACCUSATION; TWO OFFICIALS COME FROM THE IMPERIAL CAPITAL   211

Postscript 1   221

Postscript 2   225

Illustrations

JUDGE DEE   *frontispiece*

A MEETING IN A GARDEN PAVILION   3

THE YEH BROTHERS REPORT A MURDER   14

MA JOONG AND A BOXER HEAR A SOLDIER'S STORY   63

JUDGE DEE AND CORONER KUO   107

A WOMAN IS PUNISHED FOR CONTEMPT OF COURT   130

MRS. LOO ARRIVES AT THE CEMETERY   178

THE LAST MEETING ON MEDICINE HILL   209

JUDGE DEE READS AN IMPERIAL EDICT   216

Sketch Map of Pei-chow

 1 Tribunal
 2 Old Drill Ground
 3 Drum Tower
 4 Chu Mansion
 5 Kuo's Pharmacy
 6 Temple of the War God
 7 Army godowns
 8 Pan Feng's curio shop
 9 Yeh's paper shop
10 Bell Tower
11 Temple of the City God
12 Mrs. Loo's cotton shop
13 Lan Tao-kuei's house
14 Thermal bath-house
15 Covered Market
16 Temple of Confucius
17 Liao Mansion
18 Main Thoroughfare
19 Medicine Hill
20 Cemetery

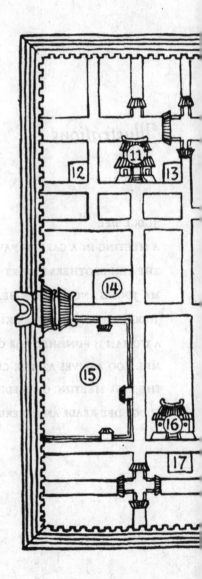

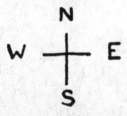

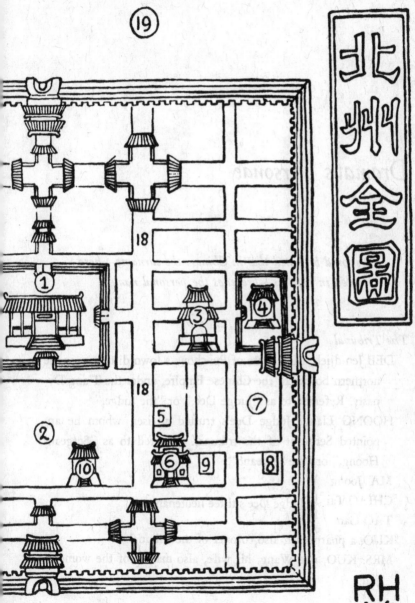

Dramatis Personae

It should be noted that in Chinese the surname—here printed in capitals—precedes the personal name.

The Tribunal

DEE Jen-djieh, Magistrate of Pei-chow, a town district near the northern border of the Chinese Empire, under the T'ang Dynasty. Referred to as "Judge Dee," or "the judge."

HOONG Liang, Judge Dee's trusted adviser, whom he appointed Sergeant of the tribunal. Referred to as "Sergeant Hoong," or "the Sergeant."

MA Joong
CHIAO Tai } Judge Dee's three lieutenants.
TAO Gan

KUO, a pharmacist, also coroner of the tribunal.

MRS. KUO, nee Wang, his wife, also matron of the women's jail.

The Case of the Headless Corpse

YEH Pin, a paper merchant.

YEH Tai, his younger brother.

PAN Feng, a curio dealer.

MRS. PAN, nee Yeh, his wife.

KAO, warden of the quarter where the crime took place.

The Case of the Paper Cat

LAN Tao-kuei, a boxing champion.

MEI Cheng, his chief assistant.

The Case of the Murdered Merchant

LOO Ming, a cotton merchant, died five months previously.

MRS. LOO, nee Chen, his widow.

LOO Mei-lan, her infant daughter.

Others

LIAO, Master of the Guild of the Leatherworkers.

LIAO Lien-fang, his daughter who disappeared.

CHU Ta-yuan, wealthy landowner and leading citizen of Pei-chow.

YU Kang, his secretary, betrothed of Miss Liao Lien-fang.

The
Chinese
Nail
Murders

First Chapter: AN UNEXPECTED MEETING IN A GARDEN
PAVILION; A FIENDISH MURDER IS REPORTED TO JUDGE DEE

*A judge must brave the foaming billows of hate, deceit, and
doubt,*
The only bridge across is straight and narrow as a rapier's edge.
*He may not lose his foothold once, once pause to listen to his
heart,*
*Heed Justice only, lodestar unfailing, though always remote and
cold.*

LAST night I was sitting all alone in my garden pavilion, enjoying
the cool evening breeze. The hour was late, my wives had retired
to their respective quarters long before.

The entire evening I had been working hard in my library,
keeping my boyservant busy getting the books I wanted from the
shelves, and making him copy out the passages I needed.

As you know I devote my leisure hours to writing a com-
pendium of crime and detection in our present great Ming Dynasty, also adding an Appendix containing the biographies of the
famous detectives of former days. I am now working on the biog-

1

raphy of Dee Jen-djieh, the eminent statesman who lived seven hundred years ago. In the earlier half of his career, when he was still serving as district magistrate in the provinces, he solved an amazing number of mysterious crimes, so that now he is known chiefly as "Judge Dee," the master detective of our illustrious past.

After I had sent my yawning boyservant off to bed, I had written a long letter to my elder brother, who is serving as Chief Secretary to the Prefect of Pei-chow, far up in the north. He was appointed to that post two years ago, leaving his old house in the next street here in my care. I wrote him about my discovery that Pei-chow had been the last post where Judge Dee served as magistrate, before he was appointed to a high office in the capital. I asked my brother, therefore, to search the local records for me; perhaps he would find interesting data on crimes solved there by Judge Dee. I knew he would do his best, for we have always been very close.

When I had finished my letter, I noticed that it was very hot in my library. I strolled out into the garden, where a cool breeze was blowing over the lotus pond. I decided that before turning in I would sit for a while in the small pavilion I had built in the farthest corner, by the side of a cluster of banana trees. I was not too keen on going to bed, for to tell you the truth there had been some domestic trouble recently when I had introduced into my household a third wife. She is a lovely woman, and also quite well educated. I fail to understand why my first and second lady took an instant dislike to her, and must grudge every night I spend with her. Now I had promised to stay the night in the quarters of my First Lady, and I must confess that I did not feel in too great a hurry to proceed there.

Sitting in the comfortable bamboo armchair, I leisurely fanned

A meeting in a garden pavilion

myself with my fan of crane feathers, contemplating the garden bathed in the cool rays of the silvery moon. Suddenly I saw the small back gate open. Who shall describe my delighted surprise when my elder brother came walking in!

I jumped up and rushed down the garden path to meet him.

"What brings you here?" I exclaimed, "why didn't you let me know you were coming south?"

"Quite unexpectedly," my brother said, "I had to depart. My first thought was to come and see you; I hope you'll excuse the late hour!"

I affectionately took him by his arm and led him to the pavilion. I noticed that his sleeve was damp and cold.

When I had made him sit down in my armchair, I took the chair opposite and looked at him solicitously. He had lost much weight, his face was gray and his eyes seemed to bulge slightly.

"It may be the effect of the moonlight," I said worriedly, "but I think you look ill. I suppose the journey down from Pei-chow was very tiring?"

"It proved difficult indeed," my brother said quietly, "I had hoped to be here four days earlier, but there was so much mist." He brushed a patch of dried mud from his simple white robe, then went on, "I have not been feeling too well of late, you know, I suffer from a searing pain here." He delicately touched the top of his head. "It goes deep down behind my eyes. I am also subject to fits of shivering."

"The hot climate here in our native place will do you good!" I said consolingly, "and tomorrow we'll let our old physician have a look at you. Now tell me all the news from Pei-chow!"

He gave me a concise account of his work there; it seemed he got along quite well with his chief, the Prefect. But when he

4

came to his private affairs he looked worried. His First Lady had been acting rather strangely recently, he said. Her attitude to him had changed, he did not know why. He gave me to understand that there was some connection between this and his sudden departure. He started to shiver violently, and I did not press him further for details about a problem which evidently caused him much distress.

To divert his thoughts I brought up the subject of Judge Dee, telling him about the letter I had just written.

"Oh yes," my brother said, "in Pei-chow they tell a weird old tale about three dark mysteries that Judge Dee solved when he was serving there as magistrate. Having been handed down for generations, and being told and retold in the tea houses, this story has of course been much embellished by fancy."

"It is only just past midnight," I said excitedly. "If it doesn't tire you too much, I wish you would tell me the tale!"

My brother's haggard face twitched in pain. But when I hurriedly started to apologize for my unreasonable request, he stopped me with his raised hand.

"It may be of advantage to you to hear that strange story," he said gravely. "If I myself had given it more attention earlier, maybe things would have turned out differently. . . ."

His voice trailed off, again he lightly touched the crown of his head. Then he resumed:

"Well, you know of course that in Judge Dee's day, after our victorious campaign against the Tartars, the northern frontier of our Empire had been moved for the first time farther out in the plains north of Pei-chow. At present Pei-chow is a prosperous, densely populated prefecture, the busy trade center of the northern provinces. But at that time it was still a rather isolated district; among the sparse population there were many families of mixed Tartar blood, who still practiced in secret the weird rites of the barbarian sorcerers. Farther north the great Northern Army of Generalissimo Wen Lo was stationed, to protect the T'ang Empire against new invasions by the Tartar hordes."

After these preliminaries my brother started upon an uncanny narrative. The fourth night watch had sounded when he finally rose and said he had to go.

I wanted to accompany him home, for he was shivering badly now and his hoarse voice had become so weak that I could hardly hear what he said. But he resolutely refused, and we parted at my garden gate.

I felt in no mood for sleep, and returned to my library. There I hastily started to write the weird tale my brother had told me. When the red glow of dawn was in the sky I put down my writing brush and lay down on the bamboo couch out on the veranda.

When I woke up the time for the noon meal was approaching. I had my boyservant bring my rice out to the veranda, and ate with gusto, for once anticipating with pleasure the announced visit of my First Lady. I would triumphantly cut short her harangue about my not joining her during the night by adducing the unassailable excuse of my elder brother's unexpected arrival. When I had thus dealt with that aggravating woman, I would walk over to my brother's house for a leisurely chat. Perhaps he would tell me then exactly why he had left Pei-chow, and I would be able to ask him some elucidation about a few points which had not been very clear in the old story he told me.

But just when I was laying down my chopsticks, my steward came and announced that a special messenger had arrived from Pei-chow. He handed me a letter from the Prefect, who regretfully informed me that four days before, at midnight, my elder brother had suddenly died there.

Judge Dee sat huddled up in a thick fur coat in his armchair behind the desk in his private office. He wore an old fur bonnet with ear flaps, but still he felt the icy draft that blew through the spacious room.

Looking at his two elderly assistants sitting on stools in front of the desk, he said:

"That wind blows in through the smallest crevices!"

"It comes straight from the desert plain up north, Your Honor," the old man with the frayed beard remarked. "I'll call the clerk to add more coal to the brazier!"

As he rose and shuffled to the door, the judge said with a frown to the other:

"This northern winter does not seem to bother you, Tao Gan."

The gaunt man thus addressed put his hands deeper into the sleeves of the patched goatskin caftan he was wearing. He said with a wry smile:

"I have dragged this old body of mine all over the Empire, Your Honor, hot or cold, dry or wet—it's all the same to me! And I have this fine Tartar caftan that is much better than those expensive furs!"

The judge thought that he had rarely seen a more wretched-looking garment. But he knew that this wily old lieutenant of his was inclined to be parsimonious. Tao Gan had been originally an itinerant swindler. Nine years before, when Judge Dee was serving as magistrate in Han-yuan, he had extracted Tao Gan from a nasty situation. Then the trickster had reformed and asked to be admitted to Judge Dee's service. Since then his wide knowledge of the ways of the underworld, and his shrewd understanding of his fellow men had proved most useful in the tracking down of astute criminals.

Sergeant Hoong came back with a clerk carrying a pail with glowing coals. He piled them on the fire in the large copper brazier next to the desk. Having resumed his seat he said, rubbing his thin hands:

"The trouble with this office, Your Honor, is that it is too large! We have never had an office that measures thirty feet square!"

The judge looked at the heavy wooden pillars supporting the high ceiling blackened by age, and the broad windows opposite pasted over with thick oil paper that faintly reflected the whiteness of the snow in the courtyard outside.

"Don't forget, Sergeant," he said, "that till three years ago this tribunal was the headquarters of the Generalissimo of our Northern Army. The military always seem to need much elbow space!"

"The Generalissimo will have plenty of that where he is now!" Tao Gan observed. "Two hundred miles farther up north, right in the frozen desert!"

"I think," Sergeant Hoong said, "that the Board of Personnel in the capital is a few years behind! When they sent Your Honor out here they evidently thought that Pei-chow was still on the northern border of our Empire!"

"You may be right!" Judge Dee said with a bleak smile. "When the Director handed me my papers, he very courteously but a little absent-mindedly said he trusted that I would handle barbarian affairs as well as I did in Lan-fang. But here in Pei-chow I am separated from the barbarian tribes over the border by a distance of three hundred miles and an army of a hundred thousand men!"

The old Sergeant angrily tugged at his beard. He rose and went over to the tea stove in the corner. Sergeant Hoong was an old retainer of the Dee family and had looked after the judge when he was still a child. Twelve years earlier, when Judge Dee was appointed to his first post as magistrate in the provinces, Hoong had insisted upon accompanying him, notwithstanding his advanced age. The judge had given him official status by appointing him Sergeant of the tribunal. The old man, devoted to him and his family, was invaluable to him as a trusted adviser, with whom he could discuss unreservedly all his problems.

Judge Dee gratefully accepted the large bowl of hot tea the Sergeant handed him. Cupping his hands around it to warm them, he remarked:

"All in all we can't complain! The people here are a sturdy race, honest and hard-working. In the four months that we have been here now, we have had, next to the routine affairs of the administration, only a few cases of assault and battery, and those were quickly settled by Ma Joong and Chiao Tai! And I must say that the military police are most efficient in dealing with deserters and other backwash of the Northern Army that strays to this district." He slowly stroked his long beard. "There is though," he continued, "that case of the disappearance of Miss Liao, ten days ago."

"Yesterday," Tao Gan said, "I met her father, old Guildmaster Liao. He asked again whether there was not any news about Lien-fang."

Judge Dee put down his teacup. Knitting his shaggy eyebrows he said:

"We investigated the market, we circulated her description among all military and civil authorities of the province. I think we did all we could."

9

Tao Gan nodded.

"I don't think the case of Miss Liao Lien-fang's disappearance is worth all the trouble we took," he said. "I still believe that she eloped with a secret lover. In due time she'll turn up with a fat baby in her arms and with a bashful husband at her side, and beg her old father to forgive and forget!"

"Remember though," Sergeant Hoong remarked, "that she was engaged to be married!"

Tao Gan only smiled cynically.

"I agree," Judge Dee said, "that the circumstances seem to point to an elopement. She went to the market with her duenna, and while standing among the dense crowd looking at a Tartar with a performing bear, she suddenly was not there any more. Since you can't kidnap a young woman in a crowd, one does indeed think of a voluntary disappearance."

The deep voice of the bronze gong echoed in the distance. Judge Dee rose.

"The morning session of the tribunal is about to start," he said. "Anyhow, today I'll look over again our records of Miss Liao's case. Missing persons are always a nuisance! I much prefer a straight murder!"

As Sergeant Hoong helped him to don his official robe the judge added: "I wonder why Ma Joong and Chiao Tai are not yet back from the hunt."

The Sergeant said:

"Last night they said they would leave before dawn to catch that wolf, and be back in time for the morning session."

With a sigh Judge Dee replaced his warm fur bonnet by his official judge's cap of black silk. Just as he was going to the door the headman of the constables came in. He said hurriedly:

10

"The people are very excited, Your Honor! This morning a woman was found cruelly murdered in the south quarter!"

The judge halted in his steps. Turning to Sergeant Hoong he said gravely:

"That was a very foolish remark I made a few moments ago, Sergeant! One should never speak lightly of murder."

Tao Gan said with a worried look:

"Let's hope it isn't that girl Lien-fang!"

Judge Dee made no comment. As he crossed the corridor connecting his private office with the back door of the court hall, he asked the headman:

"Have you seen Ma Joong and Chiao Tai?"

"They came back a few moments ago, Your Honor," the headman replied, "but the warden of the market had just come rushing to the tribunal reporting a violent brawl in a wine shop. Since he urgently asked for assistance, Your Honor's two lieutenants rode back with him straight away."

The judge nodded.

He opened the door, pulled aside the curtain and entered the court hall.

Second Chapter: A PAPER MERCHANT ACCUSES AN
ANTIQUE DEALER; JUDGE DEE PROCEEDS TO THE SCENE OF
THE CRIME

SEATED behind the high bench on the raised platform, the judge surveyed the crowded court hall. Down below more than a hundred people were assembled.

Six constables stood in two rows of three before the bench, with the headman by their side. Sergeant Hoong had taken his customary place behind Judge Dee's chair, and Tao Gan stood by the side of the bench, near the lower table where the senior scribe was arranging his writing brushes.

The judge was about to raise his gavel when two men clad in neat fur robes appeared in the entrance of the hall. They had difficulty in getting through the crowd, as a number of people accosted them with questions. The judge gave a sign to the headman, who quickly went through the assembly and led the newcomers in front of the bench. Judge Dee hit his gavel hard on the table.

"Silence and order!" he shouted.

Suddenly the hall grew still, all watched the two men, who

knelt down on the stone floor in front of the dais. The elder was a thin man with a pointed white beard, his face drawn and haggard. The other was heavily built; he had a round, broad face and wore a thin ring beard that circled his fleshy chin.

Judge Dee announced:

"I declare the morning session of the tribunal of Pei-chow open. I shall call the roll."

When the personnel had duly answered the roll call, Judge Dee leaned forward in his chair and asked:

"Who are the two men who apply to this tribunal?"

"This insignificant person," the elder man said respectfully, "is called Yeh Pin, a paper merchant by profession, and the person by my side is my younger brother, Yeh Tai, who helps me in the shop. We report to Your Honor that our brother-in-law, the antique dealer Pan Feng, has cruelly murdered our sister, his wife. We implore Your Honor . . ."

"Where is that man Pan Feng?" Judge Dee interrupted him.

"He fled the city yesterday, Your Honor, but we hope . . ."

"Everything in its own time!" the judge said curtly. "First state when and how the murder was discovered!"

"Early this morning," Yeh Pin began, "my brother here went to Pan's house. He knocked repeatedly on the door, but no one answered. He feared that something untoward had happened, because Pan and his wife are always at home at that time. So he rushed home to . . ."

"Halt!" Judge Dee interrupted. "Why didn't he first ask the neighbors whether they had seen Pan and his wife go out?"

"Their house is located in a very lonely street, Your Honor," Yeh replied, "and the houses on both sides of Pan's place are empty."

"Proceed," the judge said.

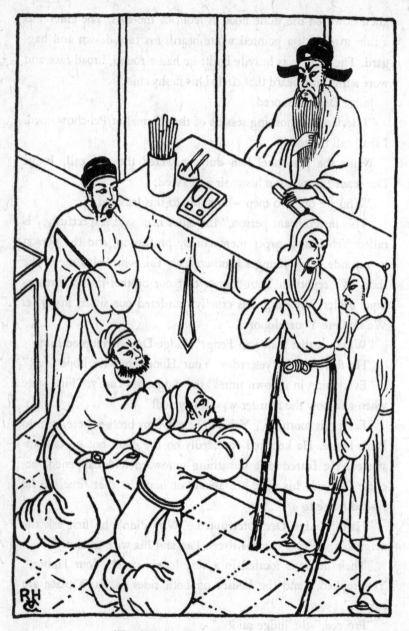

The Yeh brothers report a murder

"We went back there together," Yeh Pin continued, "the house is only two streets from ours. Again we knocked and shouted but no one appeared. Now I know that place like the palm of my hand, and we quickly walked around the compound. We climbed over the wall, and went to the back of the house. The two barred windows of the bedroom were open. I stood on my brother's shoulders, and looked inside. I saw . . ."

Emotion strangled Yeh Pin's voice. Despite the cold, sweat was streaming from his brow. He mastered himself and went on:

"I saw on the oven-bed* against the wall the naked body of my sister, covered with blood, Your Honor! I let out a cry, let go of the iron bars, and fell on the ground. My brother helped me up, and we rushed to the warden's office . . ."

Judge Dee hit his gavel on the bench.

"Let the plaintiff calm himself, and tell a coherent story!" he said sourly. "Having seen through the window the body of your sister covered with blood, how do you know that she is dead?"

Yeh did not reply, wild sobs racked his frame. Suddenly he raised his head.

"Your Honor," he stammered, "there was no head!"

Deep silence reigned in the packed hall.

Judge Dee leaned back in his chair. Slowly caressing his side whiskers he said:

"Proceed, please. You were saying that you went to see the warden."

"We met him on the corner of the street," Yeh Pin continued in a calmer voice. "I told him what we had seen and that we feared that Pan Feng might have been murdered, too. We asked

---

* In North China people use large ovens built of bricks heated by a slow fire that is kept burning inside. During the day this oven is used as a bench, during the night as a bed.

for permission to break the door open. Who shall describe our anger when Warden Kao said that yesterday he had seen Pan Feng at noon, running along the street carrying a leather sack. He said he was leaving town for a few days.

"That fiend killed our sister and fled, Your Honor! I implore Your Honor to arrest that foul murderer so that the death of our poor sister will be avenged!"

"Where is that Warden Kao?" Judge Dee asked.

"I begged him to accompany us here to the tribunal, Your Honor," Yeh wailed, "but he refused, saying that he had to guard the house and see that nobody interfered with things there."

The judge nodded. He whispered to Sergeant Hoong: "At last a warden who knows his job!" To Yeh Pin he said:

"The scribe shall now read out your plaint, and if you find the record correct, you and your brother shall affix your thumb mark to it."

The senior scribe read out his notes, and the Yeh brothers agreed it was correct. When they had impressed their thumb marks on the document, Judge Dee spoke:

"I shall proceed immediately with my staff to the scene of the crime, and you and your brother shall go there, too. Before leaving here, however, you shall give a full description of Pan Feng to the scribe to be circulated among the civil and military authorities. Pan Feng has a start of only one night, and the roads are bad, I don't doubt that he'll be arrested soon. Rest assured that this tribunal shall bring the murderer of your sister to justice."

The judge let his gavel descend on the bench and declared the session closed.

Back in his private office Judge Dee went to stand by the brazier.

Warming his hands over the fire he said to Sergeant Hoong and Tao Gan:

"We'll wait here till Yeh Pin has produced his description of Pan Feng."

"That severed head," Sergeant Hoong remarked, "is very strange!"

"Perhaps Yeh was deceived by the semiobscurity in the room," Tao Gan said. "A corner of the quilt or so might have covered the woman's head."

"Presently we'll see for ourselves what happened," the judge said.

The clerk came in with Pan Feng's full description, and Judge Dee quickly wrote out the text for the placards, and drafted a note to the commander of the nearest military-police post. He ordered the clerk: "See to it that this matter is attended to at once!"

Judge Dee's large palanquin was standing ready in the courtyard outside. The judge ascended and invited Sergeant Hoong and Tao Gan to join him inside. The eight bearers, four in front and four behind, lifted the poles on their shoulders and set off in a rhythmic gait. Two constables on horseback preceded them, and the headman followed behind with four other men.

As they entered the main street that crosses the city from north to south, the constables in front beat their small copper gongs and shouted at the top of their voices: "Make way! Make way! His Excellency the Magistrate is approaching!"

The main street was lined on both sides with shops, and there were many people about. They respectfully made way as the cortege approached.

They passed in front of the Temple of the War God, and after

17

a few turns entered a long, straight street. On the left there was a row of godowns with small, barred windows, on the right a long high wall, here and there broken by a narrow door. They halted in front of the third door, where a small group of people stood waiting.

As the bearers lowered the palanquin a man with an open, intelligent face came forward and introduced himself as Kao, the warden of the southeast quarter. He respectfully assisted the judge in descending from his palanquin.

Looking up and down the street Judge Dee remarked:

"This section of the town seems to be quite deserted!"

"A few years ago," the warden said, "when our Northern Army was still stationed here, the godowns opposite there were used for storing military matériel, and on this side of the street were eight compounds serving as living quarters of the officers. Now the godowns are standing empty, but a few families have come to live in the vacated officers' quarters, and among them were Pan Feng and his wife."

"What in the name of High Heaven," Tao Gan exclaimed, "ever made a curio dealer choose such a lonely neighborhood? You couldn't sell a bean cake here, let alone valuable antiques!"

"Exactly!" the judge said. "Do you know the answer to that, warden?"

"Pan Feng used to take his wares around to the houses of his clients, Your Honor," Warden Kao replied.

A cold blast blew through the street.

"Lead us inside," the judge said impatiently.

They first saw a large, empty courtyard, surrounded by one-story buildings.

"This area," Warden Kao explained, "is divided into units of

18

three houses. In this unit the one in the middle is occupied by Pan, the two others have been empty for some time."

They entered the door straight across the courtyard and found themselves in a large hall, sparsely furnished with a few cheap wooden chairs and tables. The warden took them across to a second, smaller courtyard. There was a well in the center, and a stone bench. Pointing at the three doors opposite the warden said:

"The one in the middle is the bedroom. On the left is Pan's workshop, with the kitchen behind it, and on the right is a storeroom."

Seeing that the door of the bedroom was standing ajar, Judge Dee asked quickly:

"Who has been inside there?"

"Nobody, Your Honor," Warden Kao said. "I saw to it that after we had broken open the door of the main entrance, none of my assistants went farther than this courtyard, so that nothing would be disturbed on the scene of the crime."

The judge nodded his approval. Entering the bedroom he saw that the left side was taken up nearly entirely by a broad oven-bed, covered with a thick, padded quilt. On it lay the naked body of a woman. It was lying on its back, the hands tied together in front, the legs stretched out stiffly. The neck ended in a ragged stump of torn flesh. The body and the quilt were covered with dried blood.

Judge Dee quickly averted his eyes from this sickening sight. Against the back wall, between the two windows, he saw a dressing table; a towel hanging over the mirror was fluttering in the icy wind that blew in through the open windows.

"Come inside and close the door!" the judge ordered Sergeant Hoong and Tao Gan. And to the warden: "Stand guard outside and let no one disturb us! When the Yeh brothers arrive, they can wait in the hall."

When the door had closed behind the warden, Judge Dee studied the rest of the room. Against the wall opposite the oven-bed stood the usual pile of four large clothes boxes of red leather, one for each season, and in the corner nearby a small, red-lacquered table. Except for two stools the room was empty.

Involuntarily his gaze went back to the dead body. Then he said:

"I don't see any of the victim's discarded clothes. Have a look in those clothes boxes, Tao Gan!"

Tao Gan opened the one on top. He said:

"There is nothing here but neatly folded garments, Your Honor!"

"Look through all four of them!" the judge said curtly. "The Sergeant will help you."

While the two set to work, Judge Dee remained standing in the center of the room, slowly tugging his beard. Now that the door had been closed, the towel hung down over the mirror. He noticed that it was stained with blood. He remembered that many people think it bad luck to look at a corpse reflected in a mirror. Apparently the murderer was one of those. A cry from Tao Gan made him turn around.

"These jewels I found in a secret compartment in the bottom of the second box," he said, showing the judge two beautiful golden bracelets set with rubies, and six hairpins of solid gold.

"Well," Judge Dee said, "I suppose an antique dealer has opportunities to get those things cheap. Put them back, this room will be sealed, anyway. I am more interested in missing clothes than in jewels that are there. Let's have a look at the storeroom."

As he saw the room stacked with packing boxes of all sizes the judge said:

"You look through all those boxes, Tao Gan. Remember that next to garments, we have also a severed head that is missing. I'll go on with the Sergeant to the atelier."

The walls of Pan Feng's small workshop were lined with shelves bearing all sorts of bowls, vases, carved jade, statues and other small antiques. The square table in the center was loaded with bottles, books, and a large collection of brushes of all sizes.

At a sign from the judge, Sergeant Hoong pulled out the large clothes.

Judge Dee opened the drawer of the table and rummaged through its contents. "Look!" he said, pointing to the heap of loose silver lying among bundles of old bills, "Pan Feng was in a mighty hurry to leave! He didn't take his jewels, nor his money!"

They had a look in the kitchen, but found nothing of any importance there.

Tao Gan joined them. Dusting his robe, he said:

"Those cases contain large vases, bronzes and other antiques. Everything is covered with dust; evidently no one has been there for at least a week or so."

The judge looked, perplexed, at his two assistants, and slowly caressed his side whiskers.

"An amazing situation," he said at last. He turned around and left the house, followed by the two men.

Warden Kao was waiting in the hall, together with the headman of the constables and the Yeh brothers.

Judge Dee acknowledged their bows with a nod, then ordered the headman:

"Let two of your men get grapples and dredge that well. Also

21

get a stretcher and blankets, and transport the body to the tribunal. Then seal the three back rooms, and leave two men on guard until further orders."

He motioned the two Yeh brothers to sit down in front of his table. The Sergeant and Tao Gan took the bench against the wall.

"Your sister has indeed been foully murdered," the judge said gravely to Yeh Pin. "There is no trace of her severed head."

"That fiend Pan took it away with him!" Yeh Pin cried out. "The warden here saw he was carrying a leather sack with a round object inside!"

"Tell me exactly how you met Pan and what he said," Judge Dee ordered the warden.

"I met Pan Feng walking very fast down the street in westerly direction," the warden said. "I asked him, 'What is the hurry, Mr. Pan?' He did not even halt for a civil reply but muttering something about leaving town for a few days he brushed past me. He looked flushed, despite the fact that he wore no fur coat. In his right hand he carried a leather sack with some bulging object inside."

The judge thought for a while. Then he asked Yeh Pin:

"Did your sister ever tell you that Pan maltreated her?"

"Well," Yeh Pin answered after some hesitation, "to tell Your Honor the truth, I always thought that they got along together rather well. Pan is a widower, much older than she, of course, with a grown-up son who works in the capital. He married my sister two years ago, and I always thought he was rather a nice fellow, though a little dull, and always complaining about his bad health. The clever devil must have been fooling us all the time!"

"He never fooled me!" the younger Yeh suddenly burst out.

"He is a mean, nasty person and . . . and my sister often complained that he beat her!"

Yeh Tai angrily puffed out his flabby cheeks.

"Why did you never tell me that?" Yeh Pin asked, surprised.

"I didn't want to cause you worries," Yeh Tai said sullenly. "But now I'll tell everything! We'll get that dog's head!"

"Why," Judge Dee interrupted, "did you go to see your sister this morning?"

Yeh Tai hesitated a moment, then answered:

"Well, I just thought I would see how she was getting along."

The judge rose.

"I shall hear your full report in the tribunal, where it can be placed on record," he said curtly. "I'll return there now, and you two shall proceed there, too, in order to witness the autopsy."

Warden Kao and the Yeh brothers conducted the judge to his palanquin.

When they were passing again through the main street, one of the constables rode up to the window of Judge Dee's palanquin. Pointing with his whip he said:

"That's the pharmacy of Kuo, the coroner, Your Honor. Shall I go in and tell him to come to the tribunal?"

Judge Dee saw a small, neat-looking shop front. The signboard bore three large, well-written characters reading, THE CINNAMON GROVE.

"I shall speak to him myself," the judge said. As he descended he added to his two lieutenants: "I always like to see pharmacies. You'd better wait outside, I don't think there is much room."

When Judge Dee pushed the door open he was met by an agreeable smell of dried herbs. A hunchback stood behind the counter, absorbed in cutting up a dried plant with a large knife.

23

He quickly came around the counter and bowed deeply.

"This person is the pharmacist Kuo," he said in a surprisingly deep, well-modulated voice.

He was only four feet high, but he had very broad, heavy shoulders and a big head with long, untidy hair. His eyes were unusually large.

"I have had no occasion yet to call on your services as a coroner," Judge Dee said, "but I have heard about your skill as a doctor, and used this opportunity for looking in. You'll have heard that a woman has been murdered in the southeast quarter. I want you in the tribunal for the autopsy."

"I'll go there immediately, Your Honor," Kuo said. Looking at the shelves stacked with jars and bundles of dried herbs he added apologetically: "Your Honor, please excuse this poor shop, everything is in such disorder!"

"On the contrary," Judge Dee said affably, "I see that everything is arranged very well." Standing in front of the large, black-lacquered medicine cupboard, he read a few of the names engraved in neat white characters on the countless small drawers. "This is a good assortment of anodynes. I see you even have the Moon Herb. That is fairly rare."

Kuo eagerly pulled out the drawer indicated and took from it a sheaf of thin dry roots. As he carefully disentangled them the judge noticed that he had long, sensitive fingers. Kuo said:

"This herb grows only on the high crag outside the north city gate. Therefore the people here call that crag Medicine Hill. We gather it in winter, from under the snow."

Judge Dee nodded. "In winter its efficiency should be at its peak," he remarked. "All the sap is then accumulated in the roots."

24

"Your Honor has expert knowledge!" Kuo said, surprised.

The judge shrugged his shoulders.

"I like to read old books on medicine," he replied. He felt something move along his feet. Looking down he saw a small white cat. It limped away and started to stroke its back against Kuo's leg. Kuo picked it up carefully and said:

"I found it in the street with a broken leg. I put it in a splint but unfortunately it did not set rightly. I should have asked the boxing master Lan Tao-kuei, he is a wonderful bone-setter."

"My lieutenants told me about him," Judge Dee said. "According to them he is the greatest boxer and wrestler they ever saw."

"He is a good man, Your Honor," Kuo said. "There aren't many like him!"

With a sigh he put the kitten down again.

The blue curtain at the back of the shop was drawn aside and a tall, slender woman entered, carrying a tray with cups of tea. As she offered him his cup with a graceful bow, the judge noticed that she had a regular, delicately chiseled face. She wore no make-up, but her face was smooth and white as the purest white jade. Her hair was done simply in three coils. Four large cats followed on her heels.

"I have seen you about in the tribunal," Judge Dee said. "I am told that you keep the woman's jail in excellent order."

Mrs. Kuo bowed again and said:

"Your Honor is too kind. There is very little work in the jail; except for now and then a female camp follower who strays here from the north, the jail is empty."

The judge was agreeably surprised by her self-possessed, yet perfectly courteous, manner of speaking.

While he sipped the excellent jasmine tea, Mrs. Kuo carefully draped a fur cloak around her husband's shoulders. Judge Dee saw the affectionate look she gave him while she knotted his neck-cloth.

Judge Dee felt reluctant to leave. The peaceful atmosphere of this small shop, pervaded by the fragrance of sweet herbs, was a welcome change after the sickening scene in the cold murder room. With a regretful sigh he put down his cup and said:

"Well, I have to be on my way!"

He stepped outside and was carried back to the tribunal.

Third Chapter: AN AUTOPSY IS CONDUCTED ON A HEADLESS CORPSE; THE JUDGE CONSULTS WITH HIS FOUR LIEUTENANTS

JUDGE DEE found the archivist waiting for him in his private office. While Sergeant Hoong and Tao Gan busied themselves over the tea stove in the corner, Judge Dee sat down behind his desk. Standing respectfully at his side, the archivist placed a sheaf of documents on the desk.

"Call the chief clerk!" the judge ordered as he started to glance through the papers.

When the clerk came in, Judge Dee looked up and said:

"Presently the headman will bring the body of Mrs. Pan to the tribunal. I won't have outsiders and idlers gaping at it, so the autopsy shall not be conducted in public. Tell your assistants to help the coroner Kuo prepare everything in the side hall here, and tell the guards that besides the personnel of the tribunal, nobody shall be admitted except the two brothers of the victim, and the warden of the south quarter."

Sergeant Hoong handed the judge a cup of steaming tea. After a few sips he said with a faint smile:

"Our tea can't compare with the jasmine tea I had just now in Kuo's pharmacy. By the way, the Kuos are a rather ill-assorted couple—but they seem happy enough together."

"Mrs. Kuo was a widow," Tao Gan said. "Her first husband was a butcher here, Wang I think his name was. He died four years ago after a drinking bout. Lucky for the woman, I would say, for I have heard that he was a mean, dissolute fellow."

"Yes," the archivist added, "Butcher Wang left large debts, also in the brothel behind the market. His widow sold the shop and everything in it, but that covered only the debts incurred elsewhere. The brothel-keeper insisted that she serve as a bondmaid with him for settling the debt, but then old Kuo stepped in. He paid the money and married her."

Judge Dee impressed the large red seal of the tribunal on the document before him. Looking up, he remarked:

"She seems quite an educated woman."

"She learned much about drugs and medicine from old Kuo, Your Honor," the archivist said. "She is a fine women's doctor now. At first people disapproved of her going about in public so freely, her being a married woman, but now they are very glad that she does. She can treat women patients much better than a man, who is of course allowed only to feel their pulse."

"I am glad she is the matron of our women's jail," the judge said as he handed the papers to the archivist. "As a rule those women are despicable harridans who must be controlled continually in order to prevent them from maltreating and cheating the inmates."

The archivist opened the door but stood aside to let pass two large, broad-shouldered men, clad in thick leather riding jackets and wearing fur caps with ear flaps. These were Ma Joong and Chiao Tai, Judge Dee's other two lieutenants.

As they strode in the judge gave them an affectionate look. Originally both had been highwaymen, "brothers of the green woods," as they are euphemistically called. Twelve years before, when Judge Dee was traveling to his first post as magistrate, they had attacked him on a lonely stretch of the road. But they had been so impressed by Judge Dee's fearless and compelling personality that they had then and there forsworn their violent life and entered the judge's service. In the ensuing years this formidable pair had proved very useful to the judge in the apprehension of dangerous criminals and other difficult and risky tasks.

"What was the matter?" Judge Dee asked Ma Joong.

Loosening his neckcloth Ma Joong replied with a grin:

"Nothing to speak of, Your Honor. Two gangs of chair-bearers got quarreling in that wine shop, and when brother Chiao and I came in they were just settling down to a real knife fight. But the two of us patted them on their heads a little, and soon after, all went home quietly. We brought along the four ring-leaders and if Your Honor approves we might let them pass the night in jail."

"That's all right," the judge said. "By the way, did you get that wolf the farmers were complaining about?"

"Yes, Your Honor," Ma Joong answered, "and a mighty fine hunt it was! Our friend Chu Ta-yuan spotted the fellow first, a large brute. But he fumbled getting the arrow on the string, and Chiao Tai put his straight in its throat! A fine shot, Your Honor!"

"Chu's fumbling gave me my chance," Chiao Tai remarked with his quiet smile. "I don't know why he bungled the shot, he is a marvelous bowman."

"And he is at it every day, too," Ma Joong added. "You should see him practice on those life-size targets he fashions out of snow! He shoots while galloping around them, and nearly every arrow hits them right in the head!" Ma Joong sighed in admiration. Then he asked: "What is that murder all the people are talking about, Your Honor?"

Judge Dee's face fell. "That is a nasty affair," he said. "You go to the side hall now, and see whether we can start on the autopsy."

When Ma Joong and Chiao Tai came back and announced that everything was ready, Judge Dee went to the side hall, followed by the Sergeant and Tao Gan.

The headman of the constables and two clerks stood waiting by the side of a high table. As the judge sat down behind it, his four lieutenants ranged themselves along the wall opposite. Judge Dee noticed Yeh Pin and Yeh Tai standing in a corner, together with Warden Kao. The judge answered their bows with a nod, then gave the sign to Kuo.

The hunchback drew aside the quilt that covered the reed mat on the floor, in front of the table. For the second time that day the judge looked down on the mutilated body. With a sigh he took up his brush and filled in the official form, reading aloud as he wrote, "The body of Mrs. Pan, nee Yeh. Age?"

"Thirty-two years," Yeh Pin said in a strangled voice. His face had a deadly pallor.

"The autopsy can begin," Judge Dee said.

Kuo dipped a piece of cloth in the copper basin with hot water standing by his side, and moistened the hands of the dead woman.

He carefully loosened the rope. Then he tried to move the arms, but they were quite stiff. He took the silver ring from the right hand, and placed it on a piece of paper. Then he washed the body carefully, examining it inch by inch. After a considerable time he turned it over, and also washed the bloodstains off the back.

In the meantime Sergeant Hoong had told Ma Joong and Chiao Tai in quick whispers all he knew about the murder. Now Ma Joong sucked in his breath.

"See those welts on the back?" he muttered angrily to Chiao Tai. "Wait till I get my hands on the fiend who did that!"

Kuo spent a long time on the stump of the neck. At last he rose and began his report:

"The body of a married woman. Skin smooth, no birthmarks or old scars. No wounds on the body, but wrists lacerated by the ropes, and bruises on breasts and upper arms. Back and hips show welts, apparently inflicted by a whip."

Kuo waited till the clerk had filled in those details. Then he continued:

"On the stump of the neck are the marks of a large knife, I presume a cleaver as is used in the kitchen."

Judge Dee angrily pulled his beard. He told the clerk to read out Kuo's report, then made the coroner affix his thumb mark to it. He ordered him to give the ring to Yeh Pin. Yeh gave it a curious look, then said:

"The ruby is missing! I am certain it was still there when I met my sister day before yesterday."

"Did your sister wear no other rings?" Judge Dee asked.

As Yeh shook his head, the judge continued: "You may now take the body away, Yeh Pin, and have it placed in a temporary coffin. The severed head has not yet been recovered; it was neither

31

in the house, nor in the well. I assure you that I shall do my utmost to apprehend the murderer and find the head, so that in due time it can be encoffined together with the body for final burial."

The Yeh brothers bowed silently, and Judge Dee rose and returned to his private office, followed by his four lieutenants.

When he entered the spacious room he shivered despite his heavy furs. He said curtly to Ma Joong:

"Put more coal in the brazier!"

While Ma Joong got busy they sat down. Slowly stroking his long side whiskers the judge remained silent for some time. When Ma Joong was seated also, Tao Gan observed:

"This murder certainly poses some curious problems!"

"I can see but one," Ma Joong growled, "and that is to get that fiend Pan Feng in our hands! Slaughtering his wife like that! And a shapely wench, too!"

Judge Dee, deep in thought, had not heard him. Suddenly he burst out angrily:

"It is an impossible situation!"

He rose abruptly. Pacing the floor he continued:

"Here we have a stripped woman, but not a single piece of her clothes, not even her shoes. She has been bound, maltreated and beheaded, and there is no sign of a struggle! The husband who allegedly did it, carefully packed up the severed head and all the woman's garments, tidied up the room, and fled—but leaving behind his wife's valuable trinkets and the silver in his drawer, mind you! Now, what do you say about that?"

Sergeant Hoong remarked:

"One would think, Your Honor, that a third person was involved."

Judge Dee halted. He resumed his seat behind the desk and looked steadily at his lieutenants. Chiao Tai nodded. He said:

"Even a strong man like an executioner, armed with his huge sword, sometimes has difficulty in cutting off a criminal's head. And we have heard that Pan Feng was a weak, elderly man. How could he have severed his wife's head?"

"Perhaps," Tao Gan said, "Pan found the murderer in the house, and got such a fright that he ran off like a hare, leaving all his possessions behind."

"There is much in what you say," Judge Dee said. "In any case we must get that man Pan as soon as possible!"

"And get him alive!" Tao Gan added significantly. "If my theory is correct, the murderer will be on his heels!"

Suddenly the door was pushed open and a spare old man shuffled inside. The judge gave him an astonished look.

"What brings you here, steward?" he asked.

"Your Honor," his old house steward said, "a messenger has arrived on horseback from Tai-yuan. The First Lady wonders whether Your Honor could spare her a few moments."

Judge Dee rose. He said to his lieutenants:

"Come and meet me here again toward dusk. Then we shall go along together to Chu Ta-yuan's dinner party."

With a curt nod he left the room, followed by his steward.

Fourth Chapter: JUDGE DEE GOES OUT TO JOIN A
HUNTING DINNER; A SUSPECT IS ARRESTED BY THE MILITARY
POLICE

SHORTLY after dark, six constables stood waiting in the courtyard with lighted lamps of thick oil paper. Seeing them stamping
their feet to keep warm, the headman said with a grin:

"Don't you men worry about the cold! You know how liberal
the Honorable Chu Ta-yuan is, he'll see to it that all of us get a
good meal in the kitchen out there!"

"And he doesn't usually forget the wine either!" a young constable said contentedly.

Then all stood at attention. The judge appeared at the door,
followed by his four lieutenants. The headman shouted for the
bearers, and the judge ascended the palanquin, together with
Sergeant Hoong and Tao Gan. As the groom brought the horses
of Ma Joong and Chiao Tai, the latter said:

"We'll pick up Master Lan Tao-kuei on the way, Your Honor!"

Judge Dee nodded, and the bearers set off at a brisk pace.

Leaning back against the cushions Judge Dee said:

"That messenger from Tai-yuan brought disturbing news. My first wife's mother is gravely ill, and she decided to leave tomorrow morning. My second and third wives will accompany her, together with my children. It won't be an easy journey this time of the year, but it can't be helped. The Old Lady is over seventy now, and my wife is very worried."

Sergeant Hoong and Tao Gan expressed their sympathy. The judge thanked them, then continued:

"It is very inconvenient that tonight I have to go to Chu Ta-yuan's dinner. The guards are bringing three tilt carts to the tribunal for transporting my family; I would have liked to be there to supervise the packing and loading. But Chu is the leading citizen here, I can't make him lose face by canceling my visit at the last moment."

The Sergeant nodded. He said:

"Ma Joong told me that Chu has made preparations for a formidable repast in the main hall of his mansion. He is a gay fellow; Ma Joong and Chiao Tai thoroughly enjoy the hunting parties he organizes for them—not to speak of the drinking bouts!"

"I wonder how he manages to stay so gay," Tao Gan remarked, "seeing that he has eight wives to keep the peace with!"

"Well," Judge Dee said reprovingly, "you know that he has no children. It must worry him greatly that he can't beget a son to continue his family. He is quite an athletic man but I don't think he keeps that harem just for his amusement."

"Chu Ta-yuan is very wealthy," Sergeant Hoong said philosophically, "but there are things even his wealth can't buy!" After a while he added: "With Your Honor's ladies and children all gone, I fear it will be very lonely for Your Honor these coming days!"

"With that murder case pending in the tribunal," the judge replied, "I don't think I would have much time for my family anyway. During their absence I shall eat and sleep in my office. Don't forget to tell that to the chief clerk, Sergeant!"

He looked out of the window and saw the black mass of the Drum Tower looming against the starry winter sky.

"We'll soon be there!" he said.

The bearers halted in front of an imposing gate. The high, red-lacquered doors swung open, and a very tall and heavy man, swathed in costly sable furs, came forward and helped the judge descend from his palanquin. He had a broad, florid face and a neatly trimmed black beard.

After Chu Ta-yuan had welcomed the judge, two other men made their bows. Judge Dee recognized with dismay the old guild-master Liao with his thin face and quavering gray goatee. He reflected that during the dinner Liao would certainly question him about the progress made in locating his lost daughter. The young man standing next to him was Yü Kang, Chu's secretary. Seeing his pallid, nervous face, the judge knew that he also would doubt-less ask news about his fiancée.

Judge Dee was still more dismayed when Chu, instead of taking them to the large reception hall inside, led them to an open terrace in the southern wing.

"I had planned," Chu Ta-yuan said boisterously, "to offer Your Honor a dinner in the hall, but we are but simple northern peasants here, you know; we could never compete with the cooking Your Honor gets at home! I thought Your Honor would much prefer to have a real hunter's dinner out in the open. Roasted meat and rustic liquor, just country fare, you know, but not entirely without taste, I hope!"

The judge made a polite reply but secretly he thought this idea of Chu's a most unfortunate one. The wind had subsided, and high screens of felt stood all around the terrace, but it was still very cold. The judge shivered. His throat was feeling sore. He thought he must have caught a bad cold that morning in Pan's house, and would have much preferred a comfortable dinner in the warm hall.

The terrace was lighted by numerous torches; their flickering light shone on a large square formed by four tables, thick boards placed on trestles. In the center stood an enormous brazier, heaped with glowing coals. Three servants stood around it, roasting pieces of meat on long iron forks.

Chu Ta-yuan made the judge sit down on a campstool at the head of the table, between himself and Master Liao. Sergeant Hoong and Tao Gan were placed at the table on the right, together with Chu's secretary, Yü Kang, opposite two elderly men whom Chu introduced as the masters of the guilds of the paper merchants and wine dealers. Ma Joong and Chiao Tai sat at the table opposite the judge, with the boxing master Lan Tao-kuei.

Judge Dee looked with interest at the famous boxer, the champion of the northern provinces. The light shone on his closely shaved head and face. The boxer had shaved off all hair so as not to be encumbered by it while fighting. The judge knew from the enthusiastic tales of Ma Joong and Chiao Tai that Lan devoted himself entirely to his art; he had never married and he lived a most austere life. While making the usual polite conversation with Chu, Judge Dee reflected that he was glad that Ma Joong and

Chiao Tai had found in Pei-chow such congenial friends in Chu Ta-yuan and Lan Tao-kuei.

Chu proposed a toast to the judge, which he had to return, although the raw liquor hurt his aching throat.

Then Chu inquired after the murder, and Judge Dee gave him a brief account, in between tastes of the roasted meat. But the fat made his stomach turn. He tried to pick up some vegetables but found it difficult to handle the chopsticks as the others did with gloves on. He impatiently pulled them off, but then his fingers froze and made eating still more difficult.

"That murder," Chu said in a hoarse whisper, "has greatly disturbed our friend, Liao, here. He fears that his daughter Lien-fang may have met with a similar sad fate. Couldn't Your Honor cheer him up a bit?"

Judge Dee said a few words to Master Liao about the efforts made to locate his daughter, but that encouraged the gray-beard to launch upon a long account of her excellent qualities. The judge felt much sympathy for the old gentleman, but he had heard his story several times in the tribunal, and he had a splitting headache. His face was glowing, but his back and legs were ice-cold. He wondered unhappily whether his wives and children would not have a very uncomfortable journey in this weather.

Chu again leaned over to the judge, and said:

"I do hope that Your Honor will find that girl, either dead or alive! My secretary is fretting himself to death about her; I quite understand, mind you, for she is his fiancée, and a fine wench. But there is much work to do on my property, you know, and the fellow really hasn't been much use, of late!"

Whispering at his ear, Chu enveloped the judge in a smell of liquor and garlic. He suddenly felt sick. He murmured that everything possible was being done to find Miss Liao, then rose and asked to be excused for a moment.

At a sign from Chu, a servant with a lamp led Judge Dee inside. Through a maze of dark corridors they reached a small courtyard with a row of washrooms at its back. Judge Dee quickly entered one of them.

When he came out another servant stood waiting for him with a copper basin of hot water. The judge rubbed his face and neck with a hot towel, and felt somewhat better.

"You needn't wait!" he told the servant, "I remember the way."

He started pacing the moonlit courtyard. It was very quiet there. The judge thought he must be somewhere at the back of this vast mansion.

After a while he decided to rejoin the party. But inside the house the corridors were pitch-dark and he soon found he had lost his bearings. He clapped his hands to summon a servant, but no one answered. Apparently all the servants were out on the terrace serving the dinner.

Peering ahead he saw a faint streak of light. Carefully walking on he came to a door standing ajar. It gave onto a small garden, surrounded by a high wooden fence. It was empty except for a few shrubs in the farthest corner, near the back door. The branches were weighed down by a thick coat of frozen snow.

Looking out over this garden, Judge Dee suddenly felt afraid.

"I must really be getting ill!" he muttered. "What is there to be afraid of in this peaceful back garden?" He forced himself to descend the wooden steps, and walked across the garden to the back door. The only sound he heard was the crunching of the snow under his boots. But he felt positively afraid now; the uncanny feeling of a hidden menace was upon him. He involuntarily halted in his steps, and looked around. His heart stood still. A strange white figure was sitting motionless under the shrubs.

Standing stock-still, the judge stared at it in horror. Then he sighed with relief. It was a snowman, made to resemble a life-size Buddhist priest sitting cross-legged against the fence, in meditation.

The judge wanted to laugh, but the smile froze on his lips. The two pieces of charcoal that represented the snowman's eyes had disappeared, and the empty sockets fixed him with an evil leer. There emanated from the figure an oppressive atmosphere of death and decay.

Sudden panic seized the judge. He turned and quickly walked back to the house. He stumbled while climbing the steps, and hurt his shin. But he walked ahead as fast as he could, feeling along the wall of the dark corridor.

After two turns he met a servant with a lamp, and he was led back to the terrace.

The diners, in high spirits, were lustily intoning a hunting song. Chu Ta-yuan was beating the measure with his chopsticks. As he saw the judge Chu quickly rose. He said anxiously:

"Your Honor doesn't look too well!"

"I must have caught a bad cold," Judge Dee said with a forced smile, "and imagine, a snowman in your back yard gave me quite a fright!"

Chu laughed loudly.

"I'll tell the servants that their children may make only funny snowmen," he said. "Here, another drink will do Your Honor good!"

Suddenly the steward appeared on the terrace, leading a squat man whose pointed helmet, short mail-coat and baggy leather trousers proclaimed him to be a corporal of the mounted military police. He stood stiffly at attention in front of the judge, and said in a clipped voice:

"I have the honor to report that my patrol has arrested the man Pan Feng six miles south of Five Rams Village, two miles east of the main road. Just now I delivered him to the warden of the jail in Your Honor's tribunal."

"Excellent work!" Judge Dee exclaimed. To Chu he added: "I greatly regret that I have to leave now to look into this. But I don't want to break up this splendid feast. I'll take along only Sergeant Hoong."

Chu Ta-yuan and the other guests conducted the judge to the front courtyard, where he took leave of his host, apologizing again for his abrupt departure.

"Duty comes first!" Chu said heartily. "And I am glad that the scoundrel has been caught!"

When they were back in the tribunal Judge Dee said curtly to Hoong:

"Call the warden of the jail."

The warden appeared and greeted the judge.

"What did you find on the prisoner?" Judge Dee asked him.

"He carried no weapons, Your Honor, only his pass and small money."

"He didn't have a leather bag with him?"

"No, Your Honor."

The judge nodded and told the warden to lead them to the jail.

When the warden unlocked the iron door of a small cell and lifted his lantern, the man who was sitting on the bench rose with a clanking of heavy chains. Judge Dee thought that at first sight Pan Feng looked like a rather inoffensive old man. He had an

41

egg-shaped head with tousled gray hair, and a drooping mustache. His face was disfigured by a red welt across his left cheek. Pan did not start upon the usual protestations of innocence but looked at the judge in respectful silence.

Folding his arms in his wide sleeves Judge Dee said sternly:

"A very serious accusation has been brought against you in the tribunal, Pan Feng."

Pan said with a sigh:

"I can easily imagine what happened, Your Honor. My wife's brother Yeh Tai must have brought a false charge against me. That good-for-nothing is always bothering me for money and of late I have resolutely refused to lend him any more. I suppose this is his revenge."

"As you know," the judge said evenly, "the law doesn't allow me to question a prisoner in private. But it might spare you embarrassment in court tomorrow if you now told me whether you have had any serious quarrels with your wife lately."

"So she is in it, too!" Pan remarked bitterly. "Now I understand why she has been behaving so strangely these last weeks, going out at unusual hours. No doubt she was helping Yeh Tai to concoct the false accusation. When day before yesterday I . . ."

Judge Dee raised his hand.

"You'll tell the full story tomorrow," he said curtly. He turned around and left the jail.

Fifth Chapter: TAO GAN TELLS ABOUT A CHAMPION'S HOBBY; A CURIO DEALER IS HEARD IN THE TRIBUNAL

THE next morning Judge Dee entered his private office shortly before the hour of the morning session. He found his four lieutenants waiting for him.

Sergeant Hoong saw that the judge was still looking very pale and tired. He had been busy till deep in the night, supervising the loading of the tilt carts. As he sat down behind his desk Judge Dee said:

"Well, my family is off. The military escort arrived before dawn. If there's no new snowfall, they should reach Tai-yuan in about three days."

He passed his hand wearily over his eyes. Then he continued in a brisk voice:

"Last night I briefly interviewed Pan Feng. My first impression is that our theory is right and that a third person murdered his wife. Unless he is a consummate actor, he has not the faintest idea of what happened."

43

"Where did Pan run off to, day before yesterday?" Tao Gan asked.

"We'll hear that presently when I question him in the tribunal," Judge Dee said. He slowly sipped the hot tea that the Sergeant had offered him, then went on:

"Yesterday night I told you three not to leave Chu's dinner, not only because I didn't want to spoil the party, but also because I vaguely felt something queer in the air. I was feeling rather ill, so it may have been my imagination. But I would like to hear whether you people noticed anything unusual after my departure."

Ma Joong looked at Chiao Tai. He scratched his head, then said ruefully:

"I must confess, Your Honor, that I had just a little too much of that liquor. I didn't notice anything particular. But brother Chiao may have more to tell."

"I can only say," Chiao Tai said with a wan smile, "that everybody was in a very happy mood—including me!"

Tao Gan had been fingering pensively the three long hairs sprouting from his left cheek. Now he said:

"I am not very partial to that strong liquor, and since Master Lan doesn't drink at all, I spent most of the time talking with him. But that did not prevent me from keeping an eye on what was happening around the table. I must say, Your Honor, that it was just a pleasant dinner party." When Judge Dee made no comment, Tao Gan went on: "However, Master Lan told me an interesting thing. When we came to speak about the murder, he said that Yeh Pin is an old dodderer but not a bad fellow; but he thinks that Yeh Tai is a mean scoundrel."

"Why?" Judge Dee asked quickly.

"Some years ago," Tao Gan replied, "Lan taught him boxing,

but only for a few weeks. Then he refused to teach him any more, because Yeh Tai wanted to learn only a few nasty dangerous blows, and showed no interest at all in the spiritual background of the sport. Lan says that Yeh Tai is extraordinarily strong, but that his mean character precludes his ever becoming a good boxer."

"That is useful information," the judge said. "Did he tell you anything else?"

"No," Tao Gan answered, "for then he started showing me the figures he makes with the Seven Board."

"The Seven Board!" Judge Dee said, astonished. "That is just a children's toy! I remember playing with it when I was a boy. Do you mean that paper square cut up into seven pieces, with which you can make all kinds of figures?"

"Yes," Ma Joong laughed, "that's a queer hobby of old Lan's. He maintains that it is much more than just a children's game. He says it teaches you to recognize the essential features of everything you see, and is an aid to concentrating the mind."

"He can make practically anything with it you tell him to," Tao Gan said, "and at a moment's notice." He took from his capacious sleeve seven pieces of cardboard, put them on the table and fitted them together so as to form a square. "This is the way you cut the paper," he said to the judge.

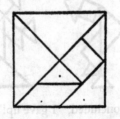

Shuffling the pieces he continued: "I first told him to make the Drum Tower, and he made this:

45

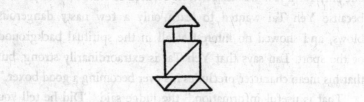

"That was too easy, so I said a running horse. That also he got immediately:

"Then I said an accused kneeling in the tribunal, and he made this:

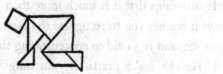

"I got sore," Tao Gan continued, "and told him to make a drunken constable and a dancing girl. But he made them!

"Then," Tao Gan concluded, "I gave up!"

Judge Dee joined in the general laughter. Then he said:

"As to my uneasy feeling that something was wrong last night, since none of you noticed anything, I assume it must have been that I was ill. Chu Ta-yuan's mansion is extraordinarily large, though. I nearly got lost in all those dark corridors."

"The Chu family," Chiao Tai observed, "has been living there for who knows how many generations. And those large, old houses often have a kind of weird atmosphere."

"It's hardly large enough for Chu to accommodate all his wives and concubines!" Ma Joong said with a grin.

"Chu is a good fellow," Chiao Tai said hastily. "A first-class hunter, and a good administrator, stern but just. His tenant farmers are devoted to him, and that proves a lot. They are all sorry for him because he hasn't yet gotten a son."

"He can't have such a bad time trying to!" Ma Joong said with a broad wink.

"I forgot to say," Tao Gan interrupted, "that Chu's secretary, that young fellow, Yü Kang, seems really very nervous. When you address him he looks as startled as if he had seen a ghost. I have a feeling that he is thinking exactly as we are, namely, that his betrothed has run away with another man."

Judge Dee nodded. He said:

"We shall have to hear that youngster before he breaks down completely. As to Miss Liao Lien-fang, her father tries so hard to convince us of her irreproachable behavior that I suspect he is trying to convince himself, too. You had better go this afternoon to the Liao mansion, Tao Gan, and try to gather some more information about that household. At the same time you can go to make inquiries about the Yeh brothers, and check on what Master Lan said about them. But don't approach them directly;

it is no use getting their wind up. Just ask the people in the neighborhood."

Three beats of the bronze gong sounded. Judge Dee rose to put on his official robe and cap.

Evidently the news of Pan Feng's arrest had spread already, for the court hall was crowded.

As soon as Judge Dee had opened the session and called the roll, he took up his vermilion brush and filled in a form for the warden of the jail.

An angry murmur rose from the audience as Pan Feng was led before the bench. The Yeh brothers, who were standing in the front row together with Chu Ta-yuan and Lan Tao-kuei, pressed forward, but the constables pushed the pair back.

Judge Dee rapped his gavel on the bench.

"Silence!" he shouted. To the man kneeling on the stone floor below he said curtly:

"State your name and profession."

"This insignificant person," Pan Feng said in a calm voice, "is called Pan Feng, an antique dealer by profession."

"Why did you leave town the day before yesterday?" the judge asked.

"A farmer from Five Rams Village, outside the northern city gate," Pan replied, "had come to see me a few days before and told me that while digging a hole in his field for burying horse dung, he had found an old bronze tripod. I know that eight hundred years ago, under the Han Dynasty, Five Rams Village was the site of a large feudal mansion. I said to my wife that it would be worthwhile to go there and have a look at the bronze. Since the sky was clear the day before yesterday, I decided to go, and come back to town the following day. Thus . . ."

Judge Dee interrupted him:

"How did you and your wife spend the morning before you left?"

"I worked the whole morning on a small antique lacquer table that had to be repaired," Pan said. "My wife went to the market, then prepared our noon meal."

The judge nodded. "Proceed!" he ordered.

"After we had eaten our noon rice together," Pan continued, "I rolled up my heavy fur coat and put it in my leather bag, for I feared that the village inn would not be heated. In our street I met the grocer, who told me that horses were scarce at the post station, and that if I wanted one I had better hurry. So I rushed along to the north gate, and was lucky enough to rent the last horse left. Then . . ."

"Didn't you meet anyone else besides the grocer?" Judge Dee interrupted him again.

Pan Feng thought for a while. Then he replied:

"Yes, I passed Warden Kao on my way to the post station, and exchanged a quick greeting with him."

At a sign from the judge he went on:

"I made Five Rams Village before dusk. I located the farm, and saw that the tripod was indeed a very good piece. I bargained a long time with the farmer without reaching an agreement with the stubborn fellow. Since it had grown late, I rode to the village inn, had a simple meal there and went to bed.

"The next morning I first made the round of the other farms inquiring about antiques, but found nothing. I had my noon meal

49

in the inn, then went back to the farmer. After another long session with him I finally bought the tripod. I quickly put on my fur coat, placed the bronze in my leather bag, and left.

"After I had ridden about three miles, however, two robbers emerged from the snow hills and came running toward me. In great fright I whipped up my horse and galloped away. Then I found that in my hurry to escape from those ruffians, I had taken the wrong road, and was lost. And to make matters worse, I noticed that the leather bag with the tripod must have dropped down, it wasn't hanging in the saddle any more. I rode around and around among the deserted snow hills, my panic growing with every minute.

"Suddenly I saw a patrol of the military police, five men on horseback. I was overjoyed at meeting them. But who shall describe my consternation when they dragged me from my horse, bound me hands and feet, and slung me over the saddle of my own horse! I asked them what it was all about, but the corporal just hit me in the face with the handle of his whip, and told me to shut up. They rode back to the city without one word of explanation, and threw me in the jail. This is the complete truth!"

Yeh Pin shouted:

"The bastard is telling a string of lies, Your Honor!"

"His statement shall be verified," Judge Dee said curtly. "The plaintiff Yeh Pin shall hold his peace until he is asked to speak!" To Pan Feng he said: "Describe those two robbers."

After some hesitation Pan Feng replied:

"I was so frightened, Your Honor, that I really did not give them a good look. I remember only that one of them wore a patch over his eye."

Judge Dee ordered the scribe to read out Pan's statement, and the headman made him affix his thumb mark to it. Then the judge said gravely:

"Pan Feng, your wife has been murdered, and her brother Yeh Pin accuses you of having committed that crime."

Pan's face turned ashen.

"I didn't do it!" he shouted frantically. "I don't know anything about it! When I left she was alive and well! I beseech Your Honor . . ."

The judge gave a sign to the headman, and Pan Feng was led away, still crying that he was innocent.

To Yeh Pin the judge said:

"When the statement of Pan Feng has been checked, you will be summoned to appear here again."

Then Judge Dee dealt with a few routine matters of the district administration, and closed the session.

When they were back in the private office, Sergeant Hoong asked eagerly:

"What does Your Honor think of Pan Feng's story?"

Judge Dee pensively caressed his side whiskers. Then he said:

"I think that he told the truth, and that a third person murdered Mrs. Pan after he had left."

"That," Tao Gan said, "does explain why the money and the gold were left untouched. The murderer simply didn't know it was there. But it does not explain the disappearance of Mrs. Pan's clothes."

"A very weak point in his story," Ma Joong observed, "is his tale about losing the bag while running away from those two robbers. Everybody knows that the military police regularly patrol that entire area for deserters and Tartar spies, and all robbers give it a wide berth."

Chiao Tai nodded.

"And all Pan could tell about their appearance," he added, "was that one had a patch over his eye. That's how our professional storytellers in the market always describe a robber."

"Anyway," the judge said, "we'll check his story. Sergeant, you'll send the headman with two constables to Five Rams Village, to question that farmer and the keeper of the village inn. I shall now write to the commander of the military-police post, inquiring about those two robbers."

Judge Dee thought for a moment. Then he added:

"In the meantime we *must* do something to locate that girl Liao Lien-fang. This afternoon, while Tao Gan goes to the Liao mansion and Yeh's paper shop, Ma Joong and Chiao Tai will go to the market, and again try to find a clue on the spot where the girl disappeared."

"Can we take Lan Tao-kuei also, Your Honor?" Ma Joong asked. "He knows that place inside and out."

"By all means," Judge Dee said. "I'll now have my noon meal, and then take a nap here on the couch. Report to me as soon as you are back."

Sixth Chapter: TAO GAN GATHERS SOME CURIOUS IN-
FORMATION; HE GETS A GRATIS MEAL FROM A RICE MER-
CHANT

SERGEANT HOONG went with Ma Joong and Chiao Tai to the guardhouse to have their noon meal together, but Tao Gan left the tribunal straightaway.

He walked along the east side of the old drill ground, covered with glittering snow. An icy wind was blowing, but Tao Gan just pulled his caftan close about his spare frame, and accelerated his pace.

Arrived in front of the Temple of the War God, he inquired about Yeh's paper shop, and was directed to the next street. He soon saw its large signboard.

Tao Gan went to the small vegetable shop opposite, and invested one copper in a pickled turnip.

"Cut it up neatly and wrap it up in a piece of good oil paper!" he told the proprietor.

"Don't you eat it here?" the man asked, astonished.

"I consider eating in the street bad manners!" Tao Gan said haughtily. But seeing the other's sour look, he added quickly: "I must say that you have a nice, clean-looking shop. I suppose you do good business here."

The man's face lit up.

"Not too bad," he replied. "I and the wife have our daily bowl of rice and vegetable soup, and no debts." Then he added proudly: "And we have a slice of meat every two weeks."

"I suppose," Tao Gan remarked, "that the big paper merchant across the street has plenty of meat every day."

"Let him," the proprietor said indifferently. "Gamblers won't eat meat for long!"

"Is old Yeh a gambler?" Tao Gan asked. "He doesn't look it."

"Not him," the other said. "It is that big bully of a younger brother of his. But I don't think he'll have much money to gamble with from now on."

"Why shouldn't he?" Tao Gan asked. "That shop looks very prosperous."

"You don't know a thing, brother," the other said condescendingly. "Now listen carefully. One, Yeh Pin is in debt, and he doesn't give one copper to Yeh Tai. Two, Yeh Tai used to borrow his pocket money from his sister, Mrs. Pan. Three, Mrs. Pan is murdered. Four . . ."

"Yeh Tai can't get any money," Tao Gan completed the sentence.

"There you are," the proprietor said triumphantly.

"That's how it goes," Tao Gan remarked. He put the wrapped-up turnip in his sleeve and went out.

He wandered about in that neighborhood, looking for a gambling club. As a former professional gambler he had a second sense for those and soon was climbing the stairs to the second floor of a silk shop.

In the large, neatly whitewashed room four men were playing dice at a square table. A squat man sat alone at a side table, sipping his tea. Tao Gan sat down opposite him.

The manager looked sourly at Tao Gan's patched caftan, then said coldly:

"Walk out again, my friend. The lowest stake in this establishment is fifty coppers."

Tao Gan took the other's teacup, and slowly ran his middle finger two times around its rim.

"Excuse my rudeness," the manager said hurriedly. "Have a cup and tell me what I can do for you!"

Tao Gan had given the secret sign of professional gamblers.

"Well," he said, "to tell you the truth I came for some confidential advice. That fellow Yeh Tai from the paper shop owes me a tidy bit of money, and he claims he hadn't got one copper now. It's no use sucking a chewed-out sugar cane, so I wanted to make sure before I put the screws on."

"Don't let him fool you, brother," the manager said. "When he came here last night, he played with silver pieces."

"The lying bastard!" Tao Gan exclaimed. "He told me that his brother is a skinflint, and that his sister who used to help him has been murdered!"

"That may be true," the manager said, "but he has other resources. Last night after he had drunk a bit he said something about milking a stupid fellow."

"Couldn't you find out who the milk cow is?" Tao Gan asked eagerly. "I grew up on a farm, I am not too bad a hand at milking, myself."

"That's not a bad idea!" the manager said with appreciation. "I'll try to find out tonight, when Yeh Tai comes along here. He has a lot of muscle, but the head-piece isn't too good. If there's enough in the deal for two, I'll let you know."

"I'll drop in again tomorrow," Tao Gan said. "By the way, are you interested in a little betting game?"

"Always!" the manager said jovially.

Tao Gan took the pieces of the Seven Board from his sleeve. Putting them on the table he announced:

"I bet you fifty coppers that I can make with these pieces anything you tell me."

Giving the pieces a cursory look, the manager said:

"Done! Make me a round copper cash, I always like the sight of money."

Tao Gan set to work, but without success.

"I can't understand this at all!" he exclaimed, annoyed. "The other day I saw a fellow do it and it looked quite easy."

"Well," the manager said placidly, "last night I saw a man here in my establishment throw a winning hand eight times in succession; that looked quite easy, too. But when his friend tried to imitate him, he lost all he had." As Tao Gan ruefully scooped up the pieces he added: "You can pay me now; you'll agree that we professionals must always set an example of prompt settlement, don't you?"

When Tao Gan nodded sadly and started to count out the coppers, the manager added earnestly:

"If I were you, brother, I'd drop that game. It seems to me that it might cost you a lot of money."

Tao Gan nodded again. He rose and took his leave. As he was

walking toward the Bell Tower he reflected dejectedly that the information about Yeh Tai was quite interesting, but at what a price.

He located the Liao mansion without difficulty; it stood near the Temple of Confucius. It was a beautiful house, with a gate richly decorated with carved woodwork. Tao Gan was getting hungry; he looked left and right for a cheap eating house. But this was a residential section; the only shop in sight was a large restaurant, opposite the Liao mansion.

With a deep sigh Tao Gan entered. He decided that this was going to be quite an expensive investigation. He went upstairs and sat down at the table facing the window, from where he could keep an eye on the house opposite.

The waiter greeted him pleasantly, but his face fell as Tao Gan ordered only a small jug of wine, the smallest they had. When the waiter brought the miniature jug, Tao Gan eyed it with distaste.

"You people encourage drunkenness, my friend," he said reprovingly.

"Look here, mister," the waiter said disgustedly, "if you want thimbles, you must go to a tailor's." Slamming a platter of salted vegetables on the table, he added: "That'll be five coppers extra!"

"I have my own," Tao Gan said calmly. He took the wrapped-up turnip from his sleeve and started nibbling it, keeping an eye on the house opposite.

After a while he saw a fat man dressed in thick furs leave the Liao mansion. He was followed by a coolie, staggering under a large bale of rice. The man looked at the restaurant. He gave the coolie a kick, barking: "Get that bale to my shop, and quick!"

A slow smile spread over Tao Gan's face. He saw the prospect of getting information and a free meal at the same time.

When the rice merchant came puffing and blowing upstairs, Tao Gan offered him a seat at his table. The fat man heavily dropped into the chair, and ordered a large pot of hot wine.

"It's a hard life nowadays," he wheezed. "If the merchandise is just a little bit wet, they return it to you. And I have a weak liver too." He opened his fur coat and tenderly laid his hand on his side.

"Not so hard for me," Tao Gan remarked cheerfully. "I'll eat rice at a hundred coppers a peck for a long time to come."

The other sat up quickly.

"Hundred coppers!" he exclaimed incredulously. "Man, the market price is a hundred and sixty!"

"Not for me," Tao Gan said smugly.

"Why not for you?" the other asked eagerly.

"Ha!" Tao Gan exclaimed. "That is a secret; I can only discuss it with professional rice-dealers."

"Have a drink on me," the fat man said quickly. And as he poured out a beaker: "Do tell me, I love a good story, you know."

"I haven't much time," Tao Gan replied, "but I'll give you the gist of it. This morning I met three fellows. They came to the city with their father, bringing a cartload of rice. Last night their father died from a heart attack; they need money quick for en-coffining the body and bringing it home. I agreed to take the whole lot, at a hundred the peck. Well, I had better go now. Waiter, the bill!"

As he rose the fat man quickly grabbed his sleeve.

"What is the hurry, my friend?" he asked. "Join me in a plate of roasted meat. Hey, waiter, bring also another pot of wine, the gentleman here is my guest."

"I don't want to be uncivil," Tao Gan said. Sitting down again he said to the waiter: "I have a weak stomach, make it roast chicken. And the largest plate."

As the waiter went away he muttered:

"First he wants 'm small, then he wants 'm big. What a waiter has to put up with."

"To tell you the truth," the fat man said confidentially, "I am a rice merchant, and I know my business. If you store that amount of rice for your own use, it'll spoil. And you can't sell it on the market, because you are not a member of the guild. I'll help you, though, and buy that lot from you at a hundred and ten."

Tao Gan hesitated. After he had slowly emptied his cup he said:

"We might talk this over. Have a drink."

He filled their cups to the rim, then pulled the platter with roast chicken toward him. Quickly choosing the best pieces, he asked:

"Doesn't that house opposite belong to Guildmaster Liao, whose daughter disappeared?"

"So it does," the other said. "But he was lucky to get rid of the wench. She was no good. But to come back to that rice . . ."

"Let's hear a spicy story," Tao Gan interrupted him, grabbing a new piece of chicken.

"I don't like to tell stories about wealthy clients," the fat man said reluctantly. "I didn't even tell my own old woman."

"If you don't trust me . . ." Tao Gan said stiffly.

"No offense meant," the other said hastily. "Well, it was this way. The other day I walk in the south section of the market. Suddenly I see Miss Liao, without a duenna or anything, coming out of a closed house there, near the wine house called The Breeze of Spring. She looks up and down the street, then quickly walks away. I think that's strange, so I walk over to the house to see who

59

lives there. Then the door opens, and out comes a thin young fellow. He also looks up and down the street, then also runs away. I ask in a shop about that house. What do you think it was?"

"A house of assignation," Tao Gan said promptly, scooping up the last pieces of salted vegetable.

"How did you know that?" the fat man asked, disappointed.

"Just a lucky guess," Tao Gan said as he emptied his cup. "Come back here tomorrow at the same time, then I'll bring the bills for the rice. We might do business. Thanks for the treat."

He briskly went to the staircase, leaving the fat man looking in astonishment at all the empty plates.

Seventh Chapter: TWO FRIENDS VISIT THE BOXER'S HOUSE; A ONE-EYED SOLDIER TELLS A SAD STORY

MA JOONG and Chiao Tai finished their meal in the guardhouse with a cup of bitter tea, then said good-by to Sergeant Hoong. In the courtyard a groom stood waiting with their horses.

Ma Joong looked up at the sky. He said:

"It doesn't look like snow, brother. Let's walk."

Chiao Tai agreed. They left the tribunal at a brisk pace.

They walked along the high wall in front of the Temple of the City God, then turned to the right and entered the quiet residential quarter where Lan Tao-kuei lived.

A sturdy youngster, evidently one of Lan's pupils, opened the door for them. He told them that the master was in the training hall.

The training hall was a spacious, bare room. Except for a wooden bench near the entrance there was no furniture. But the whitewashed walls were covered with racks holding a large collection of swords, spears and fencing sticks.

61

Lan Tao-kuei stood in the center of the thick reed mat that covered the floor. Despite the cold he was naked except for a tight loincloth. He was working with a black ball of about nine inches in diameter.

Ma Joong and Chiao Tai sat down on the bench, and eagerly watched his every movement. Lan kept the ball in continuous motion; he threw it up, caught it now on his left, then on his right shoulder, let it roll along his arm into his hand, let it drop but with one lithe movement caught it just before it touched the floor —all with an effortless grace that fascinated the two onlookers.

Lan's body was hairless like his head, and his rounded arms and legs did not show any musculature. His waist was narrow, but he had wide shoulders and a thick neck.

"His skin is as smooth as a woman's," Chiao Tai whispered to Ma Joong, "but underneath is nothing but whipcord!"

Ma Joong nodded in silent admiration.

Suddenly the champion stopped. He stood for a moment regulating his breath, then stepped up to his two friends with a broad smile. Presenting the ball in his outstretched hand to Ma Joong he said:

"Hold it a while, will you? I'll put on my robes."

Ma Joong took the ball but let it slip with a curse. It dropped to the floor with a heavy thud. It was of solid iron.

All three burst out laughing.

"August Heaven!" Ma Joong exclaimed, "seeing you working with it I thought it was made of wood."

"I wish you would teach me that exercise," Chiao Tai said wistfully.

"As I told you two before," Lan Tao-kuei said with his quiet smile, "as a matter of principle I never teach separate grips or

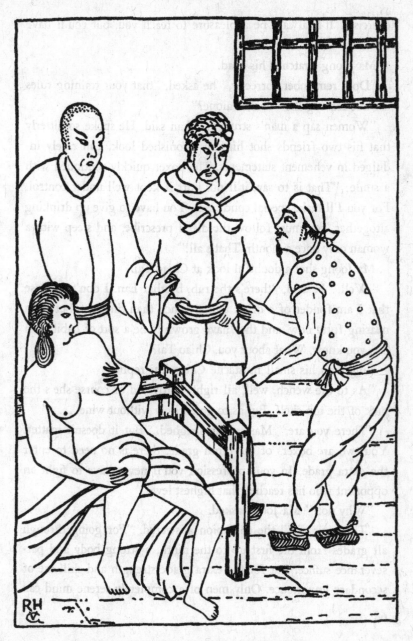

Ma Joong and a boxer hear a soldier's story

exercises. It'll always be a pleasure to teach you, but you'll have to follow the entire course."

Ma Joong scratched his head.

"Do I remember correctly," he asked, "that your training rules include leaving the wenches alone?"

"Women sap a man's strength," Lan said. He spoke so bitterly that his two friends shot him an astonished look. Lan rarely indulged in vehement statements. The boxer quickly continued with a smile: "That is to say, it'll not hurt if kept well under control. For you I'll make special conditions. You have to give up drinking altogether, you must follow the diet I prescribe, and sleep with a woman only once a month. That's all!"

Ma Joong shot a doubtful look at Chiao Tai.

"Well," he said, "there's the rub, brother Lan. I don't suppose that I am fonder of a drink and a wench than the next, but I am nearing forty now, and they have grown to be a sort of habit with me, you know. What about you, Chiao Tai?"

Fingering his small mustache Chiao Tai replied:

"As to the wench, well, all right—provided of course she's the pick of the top shelf. But as to go entirely without wine . . . ."

"There you are." Master Lan laughed. "But it doesn't matter. You two are boxers of the ninth grade, there is no need to enter the extra grade. In your profession you'll never have to fight an opponent who has reached that highest level."

"Why not?" Ma Joong asked.

"That's simple!" the champion answered. "For going through all grades from the first up to the ninth, a strong body and perseverance suffice. But for the extra grade strength and skill are of secondary importance. Only men of a completely serene mind can reach it, and that quality naturally precludes becoming a criminal."

Ma Joong poked Chiao Tai in his ribs.

"That being so," he said cheerfully, "we'd better go along as per usual, brother. Now get dressed, brother Lan, we want you to take us to the market."

While Lan was putting on his clothes he remarked:

"Now that judge of yours, I think he could make the extra grade if he wanted to. He impresses me as a man of an extraordinarily strong personality."

"That he has!" Ma Joong said. "Besides, he is a top-class sword fighter, and I once saw him hit someone so hard that it made my mouth water! He eats and drinks very moderately, and his wives we can just call routine, I suppose. Yet with him there's also a rub. You don't seriously believe that he would ever consent to shaving off that beard and whiskers, do you?"

Laughing, the three friends walked to the front door.

They sauntered along in a southern direction, and soon reached the high ornamental gate of the covered market. A dense crowd was milling around in the narrow passages, but they made way as soon as they had seen Lan Tao-kuei, for the boxer was well known in Pei-chow.

"This bazaar," Lan said, "dates from the old days when Pei-chow was the main supply center of the Tartar tribes. They say that the passages that form this rabbit warren, if put in one line, would be longer than five miles. What exactly are you looking for?"

"Our orders are," Ma Joong replied, "to find a clue to the whereabouts of Miss Liao Lien-fang, the girl who disappeared here the other day."

"It happened while she was looking at a dancing bear, I remember," the boxer said. "Come along, I know where the Tartars run that show."

He took them by a short cut behind the shops to a broader passage.

"Here you are," he said. "I see no Tartars about just now, but this is the place."

Ma Joong looked at the shabby stalls on the left and right, where the vendors were praising their wares in raucous voices. He remarked:

"Old Hoong and Tao Gan questioned all those fellows here already, and they know their job. No use asking them again. I wonder, though, what the girl came here for. You'd expect her to keep to the northern part of the market, where the better shops are, selling silk and brocade."

"What did her duenna say about that?" the boxer asked.

"She said they lost their way," Chiao Tai replied, "and when they saw the performing bear they decided to stay a while and look."

"Two streets farther south," Lan remarked, "there's the brothel quarter. Couldn't the people from there have something to do with it?"

Ma Joong shook his head.

"I investigated those brothels myself," he said, "and I found nothing. At least nothing that had a bearing on the case!" he added with a grin.

He heard a queer jabbering behind him. He turned around and saw a thin boy of about sixteen, clad in rags. His face was twitching horribly as he uttered the strange sounds. Ma Joong put his hand in his sleeve to give him a copper, but the boy had already

66

pushed past him and was tugging frantically at Master Lan's sleeve.

The boxer smiled and placed his large hand on the boy's tousled head. He calmed down at once and looked up ecstatically at the towering figure.

"You certainly have queer friends!" Chiao Tai said amazed.

"He isn't queerer than most people you see around!" Lan said calmly. "He is the abandoned child of a Chinese soldier and a Tartar prostitute. I once found him in the street; a drunken fellow had kicked him and broken a few ribs. I set them, and kept the boy with me for some time. He is dumb, but he can hear a little and if you talk very slowly he understands. He is clever enough. I taught him a few useful tricks, and now the man who dares to attack him must be very drunk indeed! There's nothing I hate more than to see weak persons maltreated. I wanted to keep the young fellow as errand boy, but at times his mind wanders and he likes it better here in the market. He comes regularly to my place for a bowl of rice and a chat."

The boy started to jabber again. Lan listened carefully, then he said:

"He wants to know what I am doing here. I'd better ask him about that vanished girl. The fellow has very sharp eyes, there's little happening here he doesn't know about."

He told the boy slowly about the dancing bear and the girl, illustrating his talk with gestures. The boy listened tensely, eagerly watching the boxer's lips. Sweat started to pearl on his misshapen brow. When Lan had finished, the boy became very excited. He stuck his hand in Lan's sleeve and brought out the pieces of the Seven Board. Squatting he began to arrange them on the street stones.

67

"I taught him that," the boxer said with a smile. "It often helps him to indicate what he wants. Let's see, what he is doing now?"

The three friends stooped and looked at the figure the boy was making.

"That's evidently a Tartar," Lan remarked. "That thing on his head is the black hood worn by the Tartars from the plain. What did that fellow do, my friend?"

The dumb boy sadly shook his head. Then he grabbed Lan's sleeve, and made some hoarse sounds.

"He means that it is too difficult for him to explain," the boxer said. "He wants me to accompany him to the old crone, a beggar woman who more or less looks after him. They live in a hole in the ground under a shop. You two better wait here. It is rather dirty and smelly there, but it's warm, and that's what counts."

Lan left with the boy. Ma Joong and Chiao Tai started to examine the Tartar daggers on display in a street stall near by.

The boxer came back alone. He said with a pleased face:

"I think I've got something for you. Come over here." He dragged the two men into the corner behind the stall, then resumed in a low voice: "The crone said that she and the boy were among the crowd watching the performing bear. They saw a well-dressed girl with an elderly lady, and tried to get to them because

68

they looked like a good prospect for begging a few coppers. But just when the old crone was going to accost the pair, a middle-aged lady who had been standing behind the girl whispered something to her. The girl quickly looked at her duenna, and when she saw that she was absorbed in the show, she slipped away with the other woman. The boy crept under the legs of the men standing there and went after them to get his coppers. But then a huge fellow wearing a black Tartar hood roughly pushed him away, and followed the pair. The boy thought he had better give up his attempt at earning a few coppers, because the hooded fellow looked very fierce indeed. Don't you think that is rather interesting?"

"It certainly is!" Ma Joong exclaimed. "Could the crone or the boy describe the woman and the Tartar?"

"Unfortunately not," the boxer replied. "I asked them, of course, the same question. The woman had covered the lower part of her face with her neckcloth, and the man had pulled the long ear flaps of his hood over his mouth."

"We'll have to report this at once," Chiao Tai said. "It's the first real clue we have to what happened to that girl."

"I'll take you to the exit by a short cut," Master Lan said.

He took them into a narrow, semiobscure passage where a dense crowd was milling around. Suddenly they heard the piercing scream of a woman, followed by the sound of breaking furniture. The people around them melted away; the next moment the three friends were alone in the passage.

"Over there in that dark house!" Ma Joong shouted. He rushed ahead, kicked the door open and entered, followed by his two companions.

They ran across a deserted sitting room to a broad wooden

staircase. Upstairs there was only one large room, on the street side. It presented a confused scene. In the center two ruffians were beating and kicking two men who lay writhing on the floor. A half-dressed woman was cowering by the bed near the door; on the bed in front of the window another woman was trying to cover her nakedness with a loincloth.

The ruffians let go of their victims. One of them, a thickset fellow with a patch over his right eye, picked out Master Lan as the weakest link in the attack, misled by the boxer's shaven head. He launched a quick blow at Lan's face. The boxer moved his head imperceptibly; as the blow glanced past his face he gave the man's shoulder a casual push. The ruffian shot forward like an arrow from the bow and fell against the wall with a crash that made the plaster come down. At the same time the other ruffian had ducked, aiming a thrust with his head at Ma Joong's stomach. But the latter raised his knee so that it hit the other right in his face. The naked woman screamed again.

The one-eyed man had gotten up. He said, panting:

"If I had my sword I'd make mincemeat out of you crooks!"

Ma Joong wanted to knock him down, but Lan laid a restraining hand on his arm.

"I believe," he said quietly, "that we are joining the wrong side, brother." To the ruffians he added: "These two men are officers of the tribunal."

The two victims, who had scrambled up now, hurriedly made for the door, but Chiao Tai quickly stood himself in their way.

The face of the one-eyed man had lit up. Looking the three friends over he instinctively addressed himself to Chiao Tai, saying:

"I regret the mistake, officer! We thought you were in with

those two touts. Me and my friend are foot soldiers of the Northern Army, on leave."

"Show your papers!" Chiao Tai said curtly.

The man pulled a crumpled-up envelope from his girdle. It bore the large seal of the Northern Army. Chiao Tai quickly looked through the papers inside. As he gave the envelope back he said:

"That is in order. Tell your story."

"The wench on the couch there," the soldier began, "accosted us in the street, and invited us to come up and amuse ourselves. We went in, and found that other wench waiting here. We paid in advance, and amused ourselves, then we had a nap. When we woke up, we found all our money gone. I started shouting, then those two slick touts appeared, and said the two wenches were their wives. If we didn't go away quietly, they would call the military police and report we had raped the women.

"We were in a nasty fix, for once the military police have you, I tell you that you go through all the Ten Hells, guilty or not. They'll beat a fellow up just to keep warm. So we decided to say good-by to our money, but first give those two bastards something to remember us by."

Ma Joong had been looking the two other men up and down. Now he exclaimed suddenly:

"Don't I recognize these two heroes! They belong to the second brothel two streets down!"

The two men immediately fell on their knees and begged for clemency. The elder one produced a money pouch from his sleeve, and handed it to the one-eyed soldier.

Ma Joong said disgustedly:

"Can't you dog's heads think up a new trick, for once? You are getting tiresome! You come to the tribunal, and the women too."

"You can file a complaint," Chiao Tai said to the soldiers.

The one-eyed man gave his comrade a doubtful look. Then he said:

"To tell you the truth, officer, we had rather not. We are due back in camp in two days, and kneeling in the tribunal is not our idea of a last good fling. We have our money back, and I must say the girls did their best. Couldn't you allow us to leave it at that?"

Chiao Tai looked at Ma Joong, who shrugged his shoulders and said:

"It's the same to me. We have those touts anyway because this is not a licensed house." He asked the elder man: "Hey you, do you rent this house also to gentlemen who bring their own bed-warmers?"

"Never, Excellency," the man answered virtuously. "It's against the law to give the clients opportunities with unregistered women. You'll find such a house in the next street, near the wine house, The Breeze of Spring. The proprietress wasn't even a member of our association. But the house is closed now, she died day before yesterday."

"May her soul rest in peace," Ma Joong said piously. "Well, then, we are about through here. We'll have the warden of the market and his men convey these two fellows and their ladies to the tribunal." And to the soldiers, "You can go."

"Thanks very much, officer," the one-eyed soldier said gratefully. "That's the first stroke of luck these last days. After that mishap with my eye we got nothing but trouble."

When Ma Joong saw that the shivering naked woman on the bed hesitated to get her clothes, he shouted:

72

"Don't be prudish, my girl! All you have is an advertisement for the house."

As the girl got down from the bed, Lan Tao-kuei turned his back on her and casually asked the soldier:

"What happened to your eye?"

"It got frozen when we were on our way here down from Five Rams Village," the soldier replied. "We looked for someone to help us to get to the city quick, but we saw only an old fellow on horseback. And he must have been a crook for he galloped away as soon as he had seen us. I said to my mate . . ."

"Halt!" Ma Joong interrupted him. "Was that fellow carrying something along with him?"

The soldier scratched his head. Then he said:

"Yes, now you mention it, he had a leather bag or something hanging on the pommel."

Ma Joong gave Chiao Tai a quick look.

"It so happens," he said to the soldier, "that our judge is interested in the fellow you saw. You'll have to come around to the tribunal, but I promise it won't take long." Turning to Master Lan he said: "Let's be on our way."

"Now that I have seen that you two fellows actually earn your pay," the boxer said with a grin, "I'll say good-by here. I'll pick up some food, then I am going to the bathhouse."

Eighth Chapter: JUDGE DEE SUMS UP TWO DIFFICULT
CASES; A YOUNG MAN CONFESSES HIS MORAL MISTAKE

WHEN Ma Joong and Chiao Tai arrived at the tribunal together with the two soldiers, the guards at the gate said that Tao Gan was back already, and now closeted with the judge and Sergeant Hoong in the private office. Ma Joong told them that soon the warden of the market would come bringing two men and two women. The men could be handed to the warden of the jail, and they were to summon Mrs. Kuo to take care of the two prostitutes. These things having been attended to, they went on to Judge Dee's office. They told the two soldiers to wait in the corridor outside.

The judge was deep in conversation with Hoong and Tao Gan, but when he saw his two other lieutenants enter he ordered them to report immediately.

Ma Joong gave a detailed account of what had happened in the market, saying in conclusion that the two soldiers were waiting outside.

Judge Dee looked very pleased. He said:

"Together with what Tao Gan found out, we now have at least a general idea of what happened to that girl. But bring those soldiers in first."

When the two soldiers had respectfully greeted the judge, he made them tell their story again in detail. Then he said:

"Your information is very important. I'll give you a letter to the military commander, proposing that you two be assigned to garrison duty in the neighboring district, so that I can summon you to deliver testimony should that prove necessary. The Sergeant shall now take you to the jail and confront you with a suspect there, then you'll go to the chancery and dictate a statement to the clerk. You can go."

The soldiers thanked the judge profusely, overjoyed to get this extension of their leave. When Sergeant Hoong had left together with them, the judge took a sheet of official letter paper and wrote the note to the military commander. Then he told Tao Gan to give Ma Joong and Chiao Tai an account of what he had learned in the gambling den and in the restaurant. When Tao Gan had finished, Hoong came back and reported that the two soldiers had immediately recognized Pan Feng as the horseman they had seen outside the city.

Judge Dee emptied his teacup, then he spoke:

"Let's now survey what we have. First, as regards the murder of Mrs. Pan. Now that Pan Feng's story about his meeting with the so-called robbers has proved true, I hardly doubt that the rest of what he said is also correct. To be quite sure we'll wait till the constables I sent to Five Rams Village are back, then we'll set Pan free. Personally I am convinced he is completely innocent. We must concentrate on getting a clue to the third person, the

man who murdered Mrs. Pan sometime between noon of the fifteenth, and the morning of the sixteenth of this month."

"Since the murderer must have known in advance that Pan
would be leaving the city that afternoon," Tao Gan observed, "he
must be someone who knew the Pans well. Yeh Tai could give us
information on Mrs. Pan's acquaintances, he was apparently very
intimate with his sister."

"We shall examine Yeh Tai in any case," Judge Dee said.
"What you heard about him in the gambling den shows that a
thorough investigation of that fellow's activities is indicated. And
I myself shall question Pan Feng about his friends and acquaintances. Now we come to the disappearance of Miss Liao Lien-fang.
Tao Gan's friend, the rice merchant, told him that she had a secret
tryst with a young man in a house of assignation in the market,
near a wine house called The Breeze of Spring. Evidently that is
the same house mentioned by the tout. A few days later a woman
accosts Miss Liao in that same neighborhood, and she slips away
with her. I presume that the woman told her that her lover was
waiting for her, therefore she immediately went away with her.
The role played by the hooded man we can only guess at."

"Evidently he was not the girl's lover," Sergeant Hoong said.
"The rice merchant described him as a thin young man, while the
dumb boy spoke about a big, burly fellow."

Judge Dee nodded. He pensively caressed his side whiskers for
some time. Then he pursued:

"As soon as Tao Gan had told me about Miss Liao's secret
meeting, I sent the headman to the shop of the rice merchant, who
is to take him to the market and point out the house. Then the
headman was to go to Chu Ta-yuan's mansion, and summon Yü
Kang. Go and see whether the headman has come back, Sergeant."

When Hoong came in again he said:

"The house which Miss Liao left was indeed the one across the street from the wine house. The neighbors told the headman that the proprietress died day before yesterday, and that the only maid employed there went back to the country. They knew that queer things were happening in that house, often there was much noise till deep in the night, but they thought it wise to pretend they didn't notice it. The headman had the door broken open. The house was better furnished than one would have expected in that neighborhood. It has been standing empty since the proprietress died, nobody has yet shown up to claim it. The headman has made an inventory, then he had the house sealed."

"I doubt whether that inventory will be very complete," the judge remarked. "Most of the movable property'll now be decorating the headman's house, I presume. I mistrust those sudden attacks of zeal of that fellow. Well, it's a pity that proprietress had to die just at this time, she could have told us much about Miss Liao's secret lover. Has Yü Kang arrived?"

"He is sitting in the guardhouse, Your Honor," replied Hoong. "I shall get him now."

When Sergeant Hoong brought Yü Kang in, the judge thought that the handsome young man was really looking ill. His mouth twitched nervously, and he could not keep his hands still.

"Sit down, Yü Kang," the judge said kindly. "We are making some progress with our investigation but I feel we should know more about the background of your fiancée. Tell me, how long have you known each other?"

"Three years, Your Honor," Yü Kang replied softly.

Judge Dee raised his eyebrows. He remarked:

"The ancients have said that when a match between two young

persons has been agreed upon, it is to the advantage of all concerned if the wedding takes place as soon as they have reached marriageable age."

Yü Kang's face went red. He said hurriedly:

"Old Mr. Liao is very fond of his daughter, Your Honor, and seemed loath to part with her. As to my own parents, since they live far away in the south, they have asked the Honorable Chu Ta-yuan to act on their behalf in all matters concerning me. I have been living in Mr. Chu's mansion ever since I came here, and he fears, quite understandably, that after I have established my own household, he will no longer be able to command my time. He has always been like a father to me, Your Honor, and I felt I could not insist on his consent to an early marriage."

Judge Dee made no comment. He asked instead:

"What do you think happened to Lien-fang?"

"I don't know!" the young man cried out. "I have been thinking and thinking, I am so afraid . . ."

The judge looked silently at Yü Kang as he was sitting there wringing his hands. Tears were flowing down his cheeks.

"Is it not," he asked suddenly, "that you fear that she has gone away with another man?"

Yü Kang looked up. Smiling through his tears he said:

"No, Your Honor, that is absolutely out of the question! Lien-fang and a secret lover! No, that at least I am sure of, Your Honor."

"In that case," the judge said gravely, "I have bad news for you, Yü Kang. A few days before her disappearance she was seen leaving a house of assignation in the market, together with a young man."

Yü Kang's face turned ashen. He stared at Judge Dee with

78

wide eyes, as if he had seen a ghost. Suddenly he burst out:

"Now our secret is known! I am lost!"

He broke down in convulsive sobs. On a sign of Judge Dee the Sergeant offered him a cup of tea. The young man greedily gulped it down. Then he said in a calmer voice:

"Your Honor, Lien-fang killed herself, and I am responsible for her death!"

Judge Dee leaned back in his chair. "Explain yourself, Yü Kang."

With an effort the youngster mastered his emotion. He began:

"One day, now about six weeks ago, Lien-fang came with her duenna to the Chu mansion to deliver a message from her mother to Mr. Chu's First Lady. The lady was taking her bath, and they had to wait. Lien-fang went to take a walk in one of the gardens, and I saw her there. My own room is located in that part of the compound; I persuaded her to go inside with me. . . . Thereafter we had a few secret meetings in that house on the market. An old friend of her duenna had a shop nearby, and the old woman did not mind Lien-fang's going to look at the street stalls alone while she had an interminable talk with the other old lady. We had our last meeting there two days before her disappearance."

"Thus it was you who was seen leaving that house!" Judge Dee interrupted.

"Yes, Your Honor," Yü Kang replied in a forlorn voice, "it was me. That day Lien-fang told me that she thought she was pregnant. She was frantic, because our shameful conduct would now become known. I also was in great consternation. I knew that Mr. Liao would probably expel her from his house, and Mr. Chu would certainly send me back to my parents in disgrace. I promised her that I would do my utmost to obtain Mr. Chu's consent to an early marriage, and Lien-fang said she would do the same with her father.

"I approached my master that same evening, but he flew into a rage and called me an ungrateful rascal. I wrote a secret note to Lien-fang, urging her to do her best with her father. Evidently Mr. Liao also refused. The poor girl must have become desperate, and killed herself by jumping into a well. And I, miserable wretch, am responsible for her death!"

He burst out in tears. After a while he said in a broken voice:

"My secret has been oppressing me all these days; every hour I expected to hear that her body had been found. And then that horrible man Yeh Tai came and said that he knew about my meeting Lien-fang in my room. I gave him money, but he wanted more every time! Today he came again and . . ."

"How," Judge Dee interrupted him, "did Yeh Tai come to know your secret?"

"Apparently," Yü Kang answered, "an old maidservant called Liu had spied on us. She had formerly served in the Yeh family as Yeh Tai's nurse, and she told him about it when they stood gossiping together in the corridor outside Chu's library. Yeh Tai was waiting there to see him on some business transaction. Yeh Tai assured me that the old woman had promised him to tell no one else about it."

"The old woman herself did not bother you?" the judge asked.

"No, Your Honor," Yü Kang replied, "but I myself tried to talk to her to make sure that she would keep her promise. Until to-day, however, I did not succeed in getting hold of her." Seeing Judge Dee's astonished look, Yü Kang quickly explained: "My master has divided the mansion into eight separate households, each with its own kitchen and its own servants. The main part of the compound is occupied by Mr. Chu himself, his First Lady, and his office, also including my quarters. Then there are separate quarters for each of my master's seven other wives. Since there are scores of servants, and since all have strict orders to keep to their own part of the compound, it is not easy for me to seek out one for a private talk.

"This morning, however, I happened to see the old woman Liu when I came out of my master's office, having talked over the accounts of the tenant farmers with him. I quickly asked her what she had told Yeh Tai about Lien-fang and me, but she pretended not to know what I was talking about. Apparently she is still completely loyal to Yeh Tai." Then he added miserably: "In any case it doesn't matter now any more whether she keeps the secret or not!"

"It does matter, Yü Kang," the judge said quickly. "I have proof that Lien-fang did not kill herself, but that she was abducted."

"Who did it?" Yü Kang cried out. "Where is she?"

Judge Dee raised his hand.

"The investigation is still in progress," he said calmly. "You shall keep your secret, so as not to give warning to Lien-fang's kidnaper. When Yeh Tai comes again to ask for money, you shall tell him only to come back in a day or two. I trust that in the meantime I shall have located your fiancée, and apprehended the criminal who abducted her by a mean ruse.

"You have behaved in a most reprehensible manner, Yü Kang. Instead of guiding that young girl, you took advantage of her affection and gratified a desire you had not yet the right to gratify. Betrothal and marriage are not a private affair. It is a solemn pact involving all the members of the two families concerned, whether alive or dead. You offended the ancestors to whom the betrothal was announced before the family altar, and you also debased your future bride. At the same time you provided a criminal with the means for getting her in his clutches, for he lured her away by falsely saying that you were waiting for her. You also wantonly prolonged the misery she must be living in now by not reporting to me the truth as soon as you learned about her disappearance. You have much to make good to her, Yü Kang! Now you can go, I shall summon you again when I have located her."

The young man wanted to speak but he couldn't manage to bring out a word. He turned around and staggered to the door.

Judge Dee's assistants broke out in excited speech. But the judge raised his hand. He said:

"This information solves the case of Miss Liao. It must be that scoundrel Yeh Tai who organized the abduction, for next to the old maid he was the only one who knew their secret. And the description the dumb boy gave of the hooded man fits him exactly. The woman he used for delivering the faked message must have been the proprietress of the house of assignation. But she didn't take her there, she must have brought her to some other secret haunt where Yeh Tai keeps Miss Liao now confined—whether for his own lust or for selling her to others we have yet to find out. He knows he is quite safe, for the unfortunate girl will now of course never dare to approach her fiancé or her parents. Heaven knows how she is being maltreated! And as if that were not enough, the brazen rascal dares to blackmail Yü Kang!"

"Shall I go now and get that sunny character, Your Honor?" Ma Joong asked hopefully.

"By all means!" Judge Dee said. "Go together with Chiao Tai to Yeh's house; the brothers will probably be eating their evening rice now. Just watch the house. When Yeh Tai goes out, you follow him, he'll take you to his secret haunt. When he is inside you arrest him and everybody else there who seems involved. You needn't be too careful while handling Yeh Tai, only don't damage him so much that I can't question him any more! Good luck."

Ninth Chapter: JUDGE DEE TAKES HOME A LOST
SMALL GIRL; HE HEARS THE NEWS ABOUT ANOTHER MUR-
DER

MA JOONG and Chiao Tai rushed out, and soon Sergeant Hoong
and Tao Gan left also to take their evening rice. Judge Dee
started to work on a pile of official papers that had come in from
the prefecture.

There was a soft knock on the door. "Come in!" he called out,
pushing the papers aside. He thought it was the clerk bringing
the tray with his evening meal. But when he looked up he saw
the slender figure of Mrs. Kuo.

She wore a long hooded robe of gray fur that suited her very
well. While she made her bow before the desk the judge noticed
a waft of that same agreeable smell of sweet herbs that pervaded
the Cinnamon Grove.

"Sit down, Mrs. Kuo!" he said, "you are not in the court hall."

As she sat down on the edge of a stool, Mrs. Kuo said:

"I made bold to come here, Your Honor, to report on the two
women who were arrested this afternoon."

"Proceed," the judge said, settling back in his armchair. He took up his teacup, but seeing that it was empty put it down again. Mrs. Kuo rose quickly, and filled it from the large teapot on the corner of the desk. Then she began:

"Both women are farmers' daughters from the south. Their parents sold them to a procurer last autumn when the crops came out so badly. He took them here to Pei-chow, and sold them to one of the brothels in the market. The owner placed them in that private house, and had them practice a few times the blackmail trick they tried yesterday.

"I don't think they are bad girls. They hate the life they are leading but there is nothing they can do about it, for the sale was in order, the brothel-owner has the receipt signed and sealed by their parents."

Judge Dee heaved a sigh.

"The old story," he said. "However, since their owner used a house without a license, we can do something. How did those scoundrels treat the women?"

"Also that is the old story," Mrs. Kuo replied with a faint smile. "They were often beaten and they had to work hard cleaning the house and preparing the food."

She adjusted her hood with a deft movement of her slender hand. The judge could not help thinking that she was indeed a remarkably attractive woman.

"The regular punishment for operating a house without a license," he remarked, "is a heavy fine. But that won't do, the owner will pay up and take it out on the girls. Since we have the charge of blackmail against him also, we'll declare the bill of sale null and void. And since you say that they are fundamentally decent girls, I'll have them returned to their parents."

85

"Your Honor is very considerate," Mrs. Kuo said, rising.

As she stood waiting to be dismissed the judge felt that he would like to prolong this conversation. Annoyed with himself he said rather curtly:

"Thank you for your prompt report, Mrs. Kuo. You can go now."

She bowed and left.

Judge Dee started pacing the floor, his hands on his back. His office seemed lonelier and colder than ever. He reflected that his wives would probably have reached the first post station by now and wondered whether their quarters there would be comfortable.

The clerk brought his evening meal, and he ate quickly. Then he rose and sipped his tea, standing near the brazier.

The door opened and Ma Joong came in, looking rather crestfallen.

"Yeh Tai went out after the noon meal, Your Honor," he said, "and he hasn't come back for dinner. A servant told me that he often eats out together with some other gamblers, and doesn't come home till very late. Chiao Tai is still watching the house."

"What a pity," Judge Dee said regretfully, "I had hoped to get that girl out of there quickly. Well, there is no use continuing the watch tonight. Tomorrow Yeh Tai will certainly come to the morning session together with Yeh Pin, and then we'll nab him."

When Ma Joong had left, the judge sat down at his desk. He took up the official documents again, and tried to resume his reading. But he found he could not concentrate. He was very annoyed that Yeh Tai had not been at home. He told himself that this irritation was quite unreasonable, why should the scoundrel have chosen this particular night to visit his secret haunt?

Yet it was awkward not to be able to take action now that the end of the case was in sight. Perhaps the fellow was on his way there this very moment, after having eaten his dinner in a restaurant. That black hood could be easily recognized in a crowd. . . . Suddenly the judge sat erect. Where had he seen such a hood last? Wasn't it in a crowd near the Temple of the City God?

Judge Dee rose abruptly.

He went to the large cupboard against the back wall and rummaged through the assortment of old clothes inside. He found a shabby, patched fur coat that seemed still good enough to keep him warm. When he had put it on he exchanged his fur bonnet for a thick scarf, which he wound tightly around his head and the lower part of his face. Then he took out the portable medicine chest that he kept in his office, and slung it over his shoulder. Looking in the mirror he decided that he could pass for an itinerant physician. He left the tribunal by the western side door.

Small snowflakes were fluttering down; the judge thought that they would soon cease. He sauntered in the direction of the Temple of the City God, scrutinizing the people who hurried past him, huddled in their furs. But he saw only fur caps, and here and there a Tartar turban.

When he had aimlessly walked about for some time, the sky cleared. He reflected that it was one to a thousand that he would meet Yeh Tai. At the same time he realized with dismay that he had not really expected to meet him, it was more that he had wanted a change. Anything was better than that cold, lonely office of his. . . . The judge was now thoroughly disgusted with himself. He stood still and looked around. He found himself in a narrow, dark street. There were no people about. He walked ahead quickly. He would go back to his office, and do some work.

Suddenly he heard a whimpering sound in the darkness somewhere on his left. Halting in his steps he discovered a small child huddled up in a corner of an empty porch. He stooped and saw it was a girl of about five or six years who was sitting there crying desperately.

"What is wrong with you, little girl?" Judge Dee asked kindly.

"I have lost the way, and I can't go home!" the girl cried out frantically.

"I know exactly where you live, and I'll take you there!" the judge said reassuringly. He put his medicine chest down, sat on it and took the girl in his arms. Noticing that her tiny body was shivering in the thin padded house robe, he loosened his fur coat and put her inside against his body. Soon the girl stopped crying. "You must first warm yourself," Judge Dee said.

"And then you'll take me home," the girl said with satisfaction.

"Yes," Judge Dee replied. "What does your mother call you, again?"

"Mei-lan," the girl said reproachfully. "Don't you know that?"

"Of course!" the judge said. "I know your name: Wang Mei-lan."

"Now you are teasing!" the girl pouted. "You know I am called Loo Mei-lan."

"Oh yes," the judge said, "your father has that shop there. . . ."

"You are just pretending!" the girl said, disappointed. "Father is dead, and Mother looks after the cotton shop. I think you really know very little."

"I am a doctor, I am always very busy," Judge Dee said defensively. "Now tell me, what side of the Temple of the City God do you pass when you go with your mother to the market?"

"The side where the two stone lions are," the girl answered immediately. "Which one do you like the best?"

"The one with the ball under his paw," the judge said, hoping that this time he was right.

"I, too!" the girl said happily. The judge rose. He slung the medicine chest over his shoulder with one hand and set off in the direction of the temple, carrying the girl in his arms.

"I wish mother would show me that kitten," the girl said wistfully.

"What kitten?" Judge Dee asked absent-mindedly.

"The kitten the man with the nice voice was talking to, the other night when he came to see Mother," the girl said impatiently. "Don't you know him?"

"No," Judge Dee said. To keep her happy he added: "Who is that man?"

"I don't know," she said. "I thought you would know him. He comes sometimes late at night, and I hear him talking to a kitten. But when I asked Mother about it she was angry and said I had been dreaming. But that isn't true."

Judge Dee sighed. Probably that widow Loo had a secret lover. They were now in front of the temple. The judge asked a shopkeeper where Mrs. Loo's cotton shop was, and the man gave him a few directions. Walking on, Judge Dee asked the girl:

"Why did you run out of the house so late?"

"I had a bad dream," she answered, "and I woke up in such a fright. Then I ran out to look for Mother."

"Why didn't you call the maid?" the judge asked.

"Mother sent her away after Father had died," the girl said, "so there was nobody tonight!"

Judge Dee halted before a door marked "Loo's Cotton Shop"; it was situated in a quiet middle-class street. He knocked, and very soon the door was pulled open. A small, rather thin woman appeared. Lifting her lantern she looked the judge up and down, then asked angrily:

"What have you been doing with my daughter?"

"She had run out and gotten lost," Judge Dee said calmly. "You should look after her better, she may have caught a bad cold."

The woman shot him a venomous look. He saw that she was about thirty years old, and quite good-looking. But the judge did not like the wild gleam in her eyes, and her thin, cruel mouth.

"Mind your own business, you quack!" she snapped. "You won't squeeze any coppers out of me."

Pulling the child inside she slammed the door shut.

"Pleasant woman," Judge Dee muttered. He shrugged his shoulders and walked back to the main street.

When he was elbowing his way through the crowd in front of a large noodle shop, he bumped into two tall fellows who seemed in a great hurry. The first one angrily gripped Judge Dee's shoulder, cursing roundly. But suddenly he let drop his hand, exclaiming:

"August Heaven! It's our judge!"

Looking with a smile at the astonished faces of Ma Joong and Chiao Tai, Judge Dee said a little self-consciously:

"I decided to have a look around for Yeh Tai, but I had to take a lost girl home. Now we can have a try together."

The drawn faces of his two lieutenants did not relax. The judge asked anxiously:

"What happened?"

"Your Honor," Ma Joong said in a forlorn voice, "we were on

90

our way to the tribunal to report. Lan Tao-kuei has been found murdered in the bathhouse."

"How was it done?" Judge Dee asked quickly.

"He was poisoned, Your Honor!" Chiao Tai said bitterly. "A foul, cowardly crime."

"Let's go there," the judge said curtly.

Tenth Chapter: THE JUDGE INVESTIGATES A COWARDLY
CRIME; HE FINDS A POISONED FLOWER IN A TEACUP

IN THE broad street leading to the thermal bathhouse an excited group of people had gathered. The warden of the market stood with his assistants in front of the gate. They wanted to stop the judge but he impatiently pulled his scarf down. Recognizing the magistrate they hastily stood aside.

In the large hall a thickset man with a round face came forward to meet them and presented himself as the proprietor. Judge Dee had never been to the bathhouse, but he knew that the hot water came from a spring, and was supposed to have medicinal properties.

"Show me where it happened," he ordered.

When the man had led them into a hot anteroom full of steam, Ma Joong and Chiao Tai started to take off their robes.

"Better take off everything except an undergarment, Your Honor," Ma Joong warned. "It's still hotter inside."

While the judge undressed, the proprietor explained that in

the corridor beyond they would find on the left the large communal pool, and on the right the ten rooms with private baths. Master Lan always used the private bath room at the very end of the corridor, because it was quiet there.

He pulled a heavy wooden door open, and gusts of hot steam blew in their faces. The judge saw vaguely the figures of two attendants, clad in coats and trousers of black oilcloth, to protect them against the hot steam.

"These two officers told all the bathers to leave," the proprietor remarked. "Here is Master Lan's room."

They entered a large bath room. Sergeant Hoong and Tao Gan silently made way for the judge. He saw that one-third of the smooth stone floor was taken up by a sunken pool full of steaming water. In front stood a small stone table and a bamboo bench. The large body of Lan Tao-kuei, completely naked, lay crumpled up on the floor, between the table and the bench. His face was distorted, it had a strange, greenish color. His swollen tongue protruded from his mouth.

Judge Dee quickly looked away. On the table he saw a large teapot, and a few pieces of cardboard.

"There's his cup!" Ma Joong said, pointing at the floor.

The judge stooped and looked at the broken pieces. He picked up the base of the broken cup. It contained a small quantity of brown liquid. Putting it carefully on the table, he asked the proprietor:

"How was it discovered?"

"Master Lan," the proprietor answered, "had very regular habits. He used to come here every other evening at about the same time. He would first soak in the water for half an hour or so, then have his tea, and do some exercises. We had strict orders

93

never to disturb him until, after about one hour, he would open the door and call the attendant for new tea. He drank a few cups, then dressed in the anteroom, and went home.''

He swallowed, then continued:

"Since all the attendants like him, one of them usually stands waiting with the tea outside in the corridor toward the time the master is accustomed to leave. Tonight he did not open the door. The attendant waited for about half an hour, then came to get me since he did not dare to disturb Master Lan himself. Knowing his regular habits I feared he had become ill. I immediately opened the door . . . and saw this!''

For a while all were silent. Then Sergeant Hoong said:

"The warden sent a man to the tribunal, and since Your Honor was out we immediately came here to see that nothing was disturbed. I questioned the attendants together with Tao Gan, while Ma Joong and Chiao Tai took the name of every bather as he left. But none of them has seen anybody entering or leaving Master Lan's room.''

"How was the tea poisoned?" Judge Dee asked.

"It must have been done in this very room, Your Honor,'' the Sergeant said. "We found that all the teapots are filled with ready-made tea from a large jar in the anteroom. If the murderer had put the poison in it there, he would have killed all the other guests. Since Master Lan never locked his door, we assume that the murderer walked in, put the poison in his teacup, and left.''

Judge Dee nodded. Pointing at a small white flower stuck to one of the shards of the teacup he asked the proprietor:

"Do you serve jasmine tea here?"

The man shook his head emphatically. He said:

"No, Your Honor. We can't afford to serve such expensive tea!''

"Pour the rest of the tea in a small jar," the judge ordered Tao Gan. "Then wrap up the base of the cup and the shards in oil paper. Be careful not to disturb that jasmine flower! Seal the teapot, and take it along also. The coroner will have to decide whether the tea in the pot also contains poison."

Tao Gan nodded slowly. He had been looking intently at the pieces of cardboard on the table. Now he said:

"Look, Your Honor, Master Lan was playing with the Seven Board when the murderer entered!"

All looked at the pieces of paper. They seemed arranged at random.

"I see only six pieces," Judge Dee remarked. "Have a look for the seventh. It must be the second small triangle."

While his lieutenants searched the floor, Judge Dee stood still, looking down at the corpse. Suddenly he said:

"Master Lan's right fist is closed. See whether there is something inside."

Sergeant Hoong carefully opened the dead hand. A small triangular piece of paper was sticking to the palm. He handed it to the judge.

"This proves," Judge Dee exclaimed, "that Master Lan worked on the figure *after* he had taken the poison! Could it be that he tried to leave a clue to his murderer?"

"It looks as if he disturbed the pieces with his arm when he fell to the floor," Tao Gan remarked. "As they are now they can't mean anything."

"Make a sketch of the position of those pieces, Tao Gan," the judge said. "We'll have to study it at leisure. Tell the warden, Sergeant, to have the body conveyed to the tribunal. Then you people had better make a thorough search of this room. I shall now go and question the cashier."

He turned around and left the room.

Having dressed again in the anteroom, Judge Dee told the proprietor to lead him to the cashier's office at the entrance of the bathhouse.

The judge sat down at the small desk near the cash box, and asked the perspiring cashier:

"Do you remember Master Lan coming in? Don't stand there fidgeting, man. Since you were here in this office all the time, you are the only man in this place who could not have committed the murder. Speak up!"

"I remember quite well, Your Excellency!" the cashier stammered. "Master Lan came in at the usual time, paid five coppers and went inside."

"Was he alone?" Judge Dee asked.

"Yes, Your Honor, he always is," the man replied.

"Now I take it," the judge pursued, "that you know most of the bathers by sight. Can you remember some of the people who came in after Master Lan?"

The cashier wrinkled his forehead.

"More or less, Your Honor," he said, "because the arrival of Master Lan, our famous boxer, was always a kind of landmark for me, dividing the evening into two parts, so to speak. First came Butcher Liu, two coppers for the pool. Then Guildmaster

Liao, five coppers for a private bath. Then four young fellows together, scalawags from the market. Then . . ."

"You know all four of them?" the judge interrupted.

"Yes, Your Honor," the cashier said. Then, scratching his head, he added: "That is to say, I know three of them. The fourth came here for the first time. It was a youngster, dressed in the black jacket and trousers of the Tartars."

"What did he pay for?" Judge Dee asked.

"The entire group paid two coppers for the pool, and I gave them their black tallies."

As the judge raised his eyebrows, the proprietor hastily took two pieces of black wood, each attached to a string, from the rack on the wall.

"This is the kind of tally we use, Your Honor," he explained. "A black tally means the pool, a red one a private bath. Each guest gives one half of his tally to the attendant in the anteroom who puts their clothes away, the other half, marked with the same number, they keep with them. When they leave the bath they give that half to the attendant, and he hands them their clothes."

"Is that the only control you have?" the judge asked sourly.

"Well, Your Honor," the proprietor replied apologetically, "we only aim at preventing people slipping in without paying, or walking off with other people's clothes."

Judge Dee had to admit to himself that one could really not expect more. He asked the cashier:

"Did you see all four of those youngsters leave?"

"I really couldn't say, Your Honor," the cashier answered. "After the discovery of the murder there was such a crowd that I . . ."

Sergeant Hoong and Ma Joong came in. They reported that

they had found no more clues in the bath room. Judge Dee asked Ma Joong:

"When you were checking out the bathers together with Chiao Tai, did you see among them a young fellow dressed like a Tartar?"

"No, Your Honor," Ma Joong replied. "We took the name and address of every one of them, and I would certainly have noticed a fellow in Tartar dress, because you don't see them often here."

Turning to the cashier the judge said:

"Go outside and see whether you can find any one of those four youngsters among the crowd in the street."

While the man was gone Judge Dee sat silently, tapping the table with the wooden tally.

The cashier came back with a grown-up boy, who stood awkwardly before the judge.

"Who is that Tartar friend of yours?" the judge asked.

The youngster shot him an anxious look.

"I really don't know, sir!" he stammered. "I noticed the fellow day before yesterday, he was loitering near the entrance here, but he didn't go inside. Tonight he was there again. When we went in, he followed behind us."

"Describe him," Judge Dee ordered.

The youngster looked uneasy. After some hesitation, he said:

"He was rather small, and thin, I would say. He had a black Tartar scarf wrapped around his head and over his mouth, so that I could not see whether he had a mustache, but I saw a lock of hair coming out from under the scarf. My friends wanted to talk to him, but the fellow gave us such a mean look that we thought better of it. Those Tartars always carry long knives, and . . ."

"Didn't you get a better look at him when he was in the bath?" the judge asked.

"He must have taken a private room," the youngster said. "We didn't see him in the pool."

Judge Dee shot him a quick look.

"That's all!" he said curtly. As the young man scurried away, the judge ordered the cashier: "Count your tallies."

While the cashier hurriedly started to sort out the tallies, Judge Dee looked on, slowly caressing his side whiskers.

At last the cashier said:

"That's strange, Your Honor. A black one, No. 36, is missing."

Judge Dee rose abruptly. Turning to Sergeant Hoong and Ma Joong he said:

"We can go back to the tribunal now, we have done all we can at this end. We know at least how the murderer went in and out of the bath room unobserved, and we have a general idea of what he looks like. Let's go!"

Eleventh Chapter: A CRUEL MURDER IS DISCUSSED IN
THE TRIBUNAL; THE CORONER REPORTS ON A SUSPICIOUS
OLD CASE

THE next day, during the morning session, Judge Dee had Kuo conduct the autopsy on the dead boxer's body. The session was attended by all the notables of Pei-chow, and every citizen who could find a place in the court hall.

When he had completed the autopsy, Kuo reported:

"The deceased died of a virulent poison, identified as the powdered root of the Snake Tree that grows in the south. Samples of the tea in the teapot, and of the tea left in the broken cup, were fed to a sick dog. The former proved harmless, but the dog died soon after he had lapped up a little of the latter."

Judge Dee asked:

"How was the poison introduced into the teacup?"

"I presume," Kuo answered, "that the dried jasmine flower had been previously filled with the powder, and then surreptitiously dropped into the cup."

"On what do you base that assumption?" the judge asked.

"The powder," the coroner explained, "has a faint but very distinctive smell, that would be all the more noticeable when it mixed with the hot tea. But if put inside a jasmine flower, the latter's fragrance would effectively conceal the smell of the poison. When I heated the rest of the tea without the flower, the smell was unmistakable, and I could thereby identify the poison."

Judge Dee nodded and ordered the hunchback to affix his thumb mark to his report. Rapping his gavel on the bench he said:

"The late Master Lan Tao-kuei was poisoned by a person as yet unknown. He was a distinguished boxer, several times in succession the champion of the northern provinces. At the same time he was a man of noble character. Our Empire, and more especially this district of Pei-chow which he honored with his presence, mourn the passing away of a great man.

"This tribunal shall do its utmost to apprehend the criminal, so that Master Lan's soul may rest in peace."

Again rapping his gavel, the judge continued:

"I now come to the case Yeh versus Pan." He gave a sign to the headman, who led Pan Feng in front of the bench. Then he said:

"The scribe shall now read out two statements concerning the movements of Pan Feng."

The senior scribe rose and first read out the statement of the two soldiers, then the report of the constables regarding their investigation in Five Rams Village.

Judge Dee announced:

"This testimony proves that Pan Feng told the truth about his movements on the fifteenth and the sixteenth. Moreover, this court opines that if he had actually murdered his wife, he would certainly not have absented himself from the city for two days

101

without concealing the dead body of his wife, at least temporarily. Therefore this court finds the evidence brought forward till now insufficient for entertaining the case against Pan Feng. The plaintiff shall state whether he is in a position to adduce more evidence against the accused, or whether he wishes to withdraw his charge."

"This person," Yeh Pin said hurriedly, "wishes to withdraw his accusation. He humbly apologizes for his rash act, which was inspired only by the deep grief over his sister's horrible death. In this case he speaks also on behalf of his brother, Yeh Tai."

"It shall be so recorded," Judge Dee said. Leaning forward and looking at the persons in front of the bench he asked: "Why has Yeh Tai not appeared before this tribunal today?"

"Your Honor," Yeh Pin said, "I can't understand what happened to my brother. He went out yesterday after the noon meal and he hasn't come back since."

"Does your brother often pass the night outside?" Judge Dee asked.

"Never, Your Honor!" Yeh Pin replied with a worried look. "Often he comes back home late, but he always sleeps in the house."

The judge said with a frown:

"When he comes back you will tell him to repair to this tribunal immediately. He must personally register his withdrawal of the charge against Pan Feng." He rapped his gavel, then announced:

"Pan Feng is now released. This tribunal will continue its efforts to locate the murderer of his wife."

Pan Feng hastily knocked his forehead on the floor several times to show his gratitude. When he rose Yeh Pin quickly stepped up to him and started to apologize.

Judge Dee ordered the headman to bring the brothel-keeper,

102

the two procurers and the two prostitutes before him. He handed the cancelled receipts to the women and told them they were free. Then he condemned the brothel-keeper and the two touts to three months in prison, to be released after a flogging. The three men started to protest loudly, the brothel-keeper loudest of all. For he reflected that a lacerated back will heal, but that it is difficult to recover the purchase price of two strapping wenches. While the constables dragged the men off to jail, the judge told the two prostitutes that they could work in the kitchen of the tribunal, pending the departure of the military convoy that would take them back to their native place.

The two women prostrated themselves before the bench and expressed their gratitude with tears in their eyes.

When Judge Dee had closed the session he ordered Sergeant Hoong to call Chu Ta-yuan to his private office.

The judge sat down behind his desk, and motioned Chu to take an armchair. His four lieutenants took their customary places on the stools in front. A clerk served tea in mournful silence.

Then Judge Dee spoke:

"Last night I did not further discuss the murder of Master Lan, because I wanted first to have the results of the autopsy, and also because I wanted to have the advice of Mr. Chu here, who has known the master all his life."

"I'll do anything I can to bring the fiend who killed our boxer to justice!" Chu Ta-yuan burst out. "He was the finest athlete I have ever seen. Has Your Honor any idea who could have done that foul deed?"

"The murderer," Judge Dee said, "was a young Tartar, or at least a man dressed up like one."

Sergeant Hoong shot a quick look at Tao Gan. Then he said:

"We have been wondering, Your Honor, why it should be that

youngster who murdered Master Lan. After all, there are more than sixty bathers on the list drawn up by Ma Joong and Chiao Tai."

"But none of them," the judge said, "could have gone in and out of Master Lan's room unnoticed. The murderer, however, knew that the attendants wear black oilcloth, and that resembles the black Tartar dress. The murderer entered the bathhouse together with the three youngsters. In the anteroom he did not hand in his tally, but walked straight on to the corridor, posing as an attendant. Remember that the steam is so thick there that one cannot see clearly who is about. He slipped inside Lan's room, put the poisoned flower in the teacup, and walked out again. He left the bathhouse probably by the servants' entrance."

"The clever scoundrel!" Tao Gan exclaimed. "He thought of everything."

"Yet there are some clues," Judge Dee observed. "The Tartar dress and the tally he'll of course have destroyed. But he must have left without noticing that Master Lan in his death struggle tried to make a figure with the Seven Board, and that figure may contain a clue to the criminal's identity. Further, Master Lan must have known the man well, and we have his general description as given by that youngster. Mr. Chu can probably tell us whether Master Lan had a pupil who was thin and rather small and wore his hair fairly long?"

"He did not," Chu Ta-yuan replied immediately. "I know them all, they are husky fellows, and the master insisted that they shave their heads. What a shame, that splendid fighter killed by poison —the despicable weapon of a coward."

All were silent. Then Tao Gan, who had been slowly twisting the three long hairs that sprouted from his left cheek, suddenly said:

"The weapon of a coward, or of a woman!"

"Lan never bothered about women," Chu Ta-yuan said contemptuously. But Tao Gan shook his head. He said:

"That may be precisely the reason why he was killed by one. Lan may have rebuffed a woman, and that causes sometimes a violent hatred."

"I know that much," Ma Joong added, "that many a dancing girl lamented that Master Lan took no notice of her, they told me so themselves. His very reserve seemed to attract the wenches, though only Heaven knows why."

"Stuff and nonsense!" Chu exclaimed angrily.

Judge Dee had been listening silently. Now he said:

"I must say that the idea appeals to me. It would not be difficult for a woman of slight build to disguise herself as a Tartar boy. But then she must have been Master Lan's mistress. For when she went into his bath room he didn't even try to cover himself up. The towels were hanging on the rack."

"Impossible!" Chu shouted. "Master Lan and a mistress! Out of the question!"

"I remember now," Chiao Tai said slowly, "that when we visited him yesterday, he did make unexpectedly a very bitter remark about women, something about them sapping a man's strength. And as a rule he was very mild in his remarks."

As Chu was muttering angrily, Judge Dee took from his drawer the Seven Board that Tao Gan had made for him, and arranged six pieces in the way they had been found on the table. He tried to make a figure by adding the triangle. After a while he said:

"If Lan were murdered by a woman, this figure might contain a clue to her identity. But he disturbed the pieces while falling down, and he died before he could add the last triangle. It's a difficult problem." Brushing the pieces aside he went on: "How-

105

ever that may be, our first task is to investigate all persons Master Lan used to associate with. Mr. Chu, I propose that you now consult with Ma Joong, Chiao Tai and Tao Gan on how to divide this work, so that each can start immediately on his allotted task. Sergeant, you'll go to the market, and question the two other youngsters about the appearance of that Tartar youth. If you do that in a friendly manner, drinking a cup of wine with them or so, they may come up with more information. Ma Joong has their names and addresses. And on your way out, Sergeant, tell Kuo to come here, I want to know more details about that poison."

After Chu Ta-yuan and his four lieutenants had taken their leave, Judge Dee slowly drank a few cups of tea, deep in thought. Yeh Tai's absence worried him. Could the scoundrel suspect that the tribunal was on his heels? The judge rose and started pacing the floor. With Mrs. Pan's murder unsolved, and now the poisoning of Master Lan, it would be a great relief to be able to settle at least the case of Miss Liao.

When Kuo came in the judge greeted him with a few kind words. He sat down again behind his desk, and motioned the hunchback to take a stool. Then Judge Dee said:

"As a pharmacist you can doubtless tell me how the murderer could have obtained that poison. It must be fairly rare."

Kuo pushed the lock of hair away from his forehead. Placing his large hands on his knees he said:

"Unfortunately it can be easily obtained, Your Honor. If used in small quantities it is a good stimulant for the heart, and therefore most pharmacies keep it in stock."

Judge Dee heaved a sigh. "So we can't hope for a clue there," he said. Placing the pieces of the Seven Board in front of him and shifting them about aimlessly he pursued: "Of course this puzzle might provide a clue."

Judge Dee and coroner Kuo

The hunchback shook his head. He said sadly:

"I don't think so, Your Honor. That poison causes an unendurable pain, and death ensues in a few moments."

"But Master Lan was a man of extraordinary will power," the judge observed, "and he was very clever with this Seven Board. He knew he could not make the door to call an attendant, so I think he tried to indicate the murderer in this way."

"It is true," Kuo said, "that he was very clever with that board. When he came to our house he often amused me and my wife by making all kinds of figures at a moment's notice."

"I fail to see," Judge Dee said, "what this figure could have been meant to be."

"Master Lan was wonderfully kind, Your Honor," the hunchback went on pensively. "He knew that ruffians in the market often pushed and humiliated me. So he went to the trouble to work out a new fighting system especially for me, adapted to the fact that I have weak legs but rather strong arms. Then he patiently taught me that system, and since then no one has dared to bother me any more."

Judge Dee had not heard Kuo's last words. Playing with the seven pieces of cardboard, he suddenly saw that he had made the figure of a cat.

Quickly he shuffled the pieces again. The poison used, the jasmine flower, the cat . . . he refused to follow this line of logic.

Noticing Kuo's astonished look he said hurriedly to cover up his consternation:

"Yes, I suddenly thought of a queer meeting I had last night. I brought home a small girl that had become lost, but her mother just reviled me. It was a widow, a most unpleasant person. From the innocent patter of the child I gathered that she must have a secret lover."

"What was her name?" Kuo asked curiously.

"She is a Mrs. Loo, and runs a cotton shop."

Kuo sat stiffly erect. He exclaimed:

"That is a nasty woman, Your Honor. I had some dealings with her five months ago, when her husband had died. That was a queer affair."

The judge was still confused by the discovery of the cat. And Master Lan visited the pharmacy often, he reflected. He asked absent-mindedly:

"What was queer about the death of that cotton merchant?"

Kuo hesitated before he replied:

"The matter was really treated a little cursorily by Your Honor's predecessor. But just at that time there had been an attack of the Tartar hordes on the Northern Army, and crowds of refugees came pouring into the city. The magistrate had his hands full and I can well understand that he did not want to spend much time on a cotton merchant who died from a heart attack."

"Why should he?" Judge Dee asked, grateful for the diversion. "The autopsy would have shown any suspicious features."

The hunchback looked unhappy.

"The trouble is, Your Honor," he said, "that there was no autopsy!"

The judge was all attention now. Leaning back in his chair he said curtly:

"Tell me the facts."

"Late in the afternoon," Kuo began, "Mrs. Loo came to the tribunal together with Dr. Kwang, a well-known physician here. The doctor stated that at the noon meal Loo Ming had complained of a headache, and had lain down on his bed. Shortly after, his wife heard him groaning. When she entered the bedroom, he was dead. She called Dr. Kwang, and he examined the corpse. She told him that her husband had often complained about his weak heart. Dr. Kwang inquired what he had eaten at noon, and his wife said he had taken very little food, but drunk two jugs of wine in order to get rid of his headache. Dr. Kwang thereupon signed a certificate stating that Loo Ming had died from a heart attack, occasioned by overindulgence in alcohol. Your Honor's predecessor registered the death as such."

As Judge Dee remained silent, the hunchback went on:

"Now I happen to know Loo Ming's brother, and he told me that when he assisted in dressing the corpse, he noticed that the face was not discolored, but that the eyes were bulging from their sockets. Since those symptoms point to a blow on the back of the head, I went to Mrs. Loo asking for more particulars. But she shouted at me and cursed me for an interfering busybody. Then I took the liberty to speak about it to the magistrate, but he said he was satisfied with Dr. Kwang's statement, and that he saw no reason for an autopsy. And there the matter ended."

"Didn't you speak to Dr. Kwang?" Judge Dee inquired.

"I made several attempts, but he avoided me," Kuo answered. "Then there were rumors that Dr. Kwang meddled with black magic. He left the city with the stream of refugees heading south, and no one has ever heard from him again."

The judge slowly stroked his beard.

110

"That certainly is a curious story!" he said at last. "Are there still some people here who practice sorcery? You know that according to the law that is a capital offense."

Kuo shrugged his shoulders.

"Many families here in Pei-chow," he said, "have Tartar blood, and imagine that they possess the secret tradition of the Tartar sorcerers. Some maintain that those people can kill other men just by reciting incantations, or by burning or cutting off the head of a picture of them. Others are said to know also the secret Taoist rites and to be able to prolong their life by having witches or goblins as lovers. In my opinion all this is nothing but barbarian superstition, but Master Lan had made quite a study of it and he told me that there was a basis of truth in their allegations."

"Our Master Confucius," Judge Dee said impatiently, "expressly warned us not to dabble in those dark arcana. I would never have thought that a wise man like Lan Tao-kuei wasted time on those weird pursuits."

"He was a man of wide interests, Your Honor," the hunchback said diffidently.

"Well," the judge pursued, "I am glad you told me that story about Mrs. Loo. I think I'll summon her and ask for more details about the death of her husband."

Judge Dee took up a paper and Kuo hastily bowed and left.

Twelfth Chapter: JUDGE DEE GOES TO VISIT MEDICINE
HILL; A WOMAN DEFIES THE ORDERS OF THE TRIBUNAL

As soon as the door had closed behind the coroner, Judge Dee threw the document down on his desk. Folding his arms he sat there, trying in vain to sort out the confused thoughts that were turning around in his mind.

At last he rose and changed into his hunting dress. A little exercise would perhaps help to clear his brain. He told the groom to bring his favorite horse, and rode out.

First he galloped a few times around the old drill ground. Then he entered the main street, and left the city by the North Gate. He made his horse step slowly through the snow to where the road went down the hill into the vast, white plain. He saw that the sky was leaden, it looked like another snowfall.

On the right two large stones marked the beginning of the narrow path that led up the crag known as Medicine Hill. The judge decided to climb up there, and go home after that exercise. He rode up the path to where it became a steep ascent, then dis-

112

mounted. He patted his horse on its neck, and tied the reins to the stump of a tree.

About to begin the climb he suddenly halted. There were fresh marks of small feet in the snow. He debated with himself whether he should go on. Finally he shrugged his shoulders, and began the ascent.

The top of the crag was bare but for one tree, a winter plum. Its black branches were covered with small red buds. Near the wooden balustrade at the other end a woman clad in a gray fur coat was digging in the snow with a small trowel. As she heard the crunching of the snow under Judge Dee's heavy boots, she righted herself. She quickly put the trowel in the basket at her feet, and bowed deeply.

"I see," the judge said, "that you are gathering the Moon Herb."

Mrs. Kuo nodded. The fur hood set off her delicate face admirably.

"I have not been very lucky, Your Honor," she said with a smile, "I have only gathered this much!" She pointed to the bundle of plants in the basket.

"I came up here for a little exercise," Judge Dee said. "I wanted to clear my thoughts, for the murder of Master Lan is weighing heavily on my mind."

Mrs. Kuo's face suddenly fell. Pulling her cloak close around her she murmured:

"It's incredible. He was so strong and healthy."

"Even the strongest man is defenseless against poison," the judge remarked dryly. "I have a definite clue to the person who committed that treacherous deed."

Mrs. Kuo's eyes grew wide.

"Who was that man, Your Honor?" she asked in a scarcely audible voice.

"I didn't say it was a man," Judge Dee said quickly.

She slowly shook her small head.

"It must have been," she said firmly. "I saw the master often because he was my husband's friend. He was always very kind and courteous, also to me, but one still felt that his attitude toward women was . . . different."

"How do you mean that?" the judge asked.

"Well," Mrs. Kuo answered slowly, "he seemed not to be . . . aware of them." A blush colored her cheeks, and she lowered her head.

The judge felt ill at ease. He walked over to the balustrade and looked down. He shrank back involuntarily. There was a sheer drop of more than fifty feet, and at the foot of the crag sharp stones were sticking up out of the snow.

Looking out over the plain below he was at a loss as to what to say next. To be aware of another person . . . this thought strangely disturbed him. He turned around and asked:

"Those cats I saw the other day in your house, are they your husband's interest or yours?"

"Of both of us, Your Honor," Mrs. Kuo replied quietly. "My husband can't bear to see animals suffer, he often brings home stray or sick cats. Then I look after them. By now we have seven of them, large and small."

Judge Dee nodded absent-mindedly. When his eye fell on the plum tree he remarked:

"That tree must be lovely when the blossoms are out."

"Yes," she said eagerly, "that may happen any day now. What poet said that again . . . something about one being able to hear the petals falling down in the snow . . . ?"

114

The judge knew the old poem but he said only:

"I remember some lines to that effect." Then he added curtly: "Well, Mrs. Kuo, I have to go back to the tribunal now."

She bowed deeply, and the judge began the descent.

While eating his simple noon meal Judge Dee thought over his conversation with the coroner. When the clerk came in with his tea, he told him to call the headman.

"Go to the cotton shop of Mrs. Loo, near the Temple of the City God," he ordered him, "and bring her here. I want to ask her a few questions."

When the headman had gone, the judge lingered long over his tea. He thought ruefully that it was probably very foolish to stir up that old affair of Loo Ming's death now that two murders were pending in the tribunal. But what the coroner had told him intrigued him. And it distracted his mind from that other suspicion that was disturbing him so deeply.

He lay down on the couch for a nap. But sleep would not come. Tossing himself about restlessly he tried to remember the full text of the poem about the falling petals. Suddenly it came back to him. It had been written by a poet of about two centuries before, and bore the title "Winter Eve in the Seraglio." It ran:

> *The lonely birds cry in the lonely winter sky,*
> *But lonelier still the heart—that may not cry.*
> *Dark memories come and haunt her from the past,*
> *Joy passes, it's remorse and sorrow that last.*
> *Oh that but once new love could still old pain:*
> *The winter prune on new year's eve in bloom again,*
> *Opening the window she sees the shivering tree below*
> *And hears the blossoms falling in the crystal snow.*

The poem was not very well known, she probably had seen only the last two lines quoted somewhere. Or was she familiar

115

with the entire poem, and had referred to it intentionally? With an angry frown the judge jumped up. He had always been interested only in didactic poetry, love songs he considered a waste of time. Yet he found now a depth of feeling in this particular poem that he had never noticed before.

Annoyed with himself he went to the tea stove and wiped his face with a hot towel. Then he sat down at his desk and started to read the official correspondence that the senior scribe had brought in. When the headman came he found the judge absorbed in this work.

Seeing the headman's unhappy look, Judge Dee asked:

"What is wrong, headman?"

The headman nervously fingered his mustache.

"To tell Your Honor the truth," he replied, "Mrs. Loo refused to come with me."

"What is that?" the judge asked, astonished. "Who does the woman think she is?"

"She said," the headman went on ruefully, "that since I had no warrant, she refused to come." As the judge was about to make an angry remark, he hastily continued: "She reviled me and made so much noise that a crowd gathered around us. She shouted there were still laws in the Empire, and that the tribunal had no right to summon a decent woman without a proper reason. I tried to drag her along, but she fought back and the crowd took her side. So I thought I had better come back here to ask Your Honor's instructions."

"If she wants a warrant, she'll get one!" Judge Dee said angrily. He took up his writing brush and quickly filled in an official form. He gave it to the headman, saying: "Go there with four constables and bring the woman here!"

116

The headman quickly took his leave.

Judge Dee started pacing the floor. What a harridan that Mrs. Loo was! He reflected that he really had been lucky with his own wives. His First Lady was a very cultured woman, the eldest daughter of his father's best friend. The fond understanding between them had always been a great comfort to him in times of stress, and their two sons were a constant source of joy. His second wife was not so well educated, but she was good-looking, had sound common sense and directed his large household most efficiently. The daughter she had given him had the same steady character. His third wife he had taken when he was serving in Peng-lai, his first post. After some fearful experience her family had abandoned her, and the judge had taken her into his house as chambermaid of his First Lady. The latter had grown very fond of her, and soon insisted that the judge take her as a wife. At first the judge had objected, he thought it would be taking advantage of her gratitude. But when she had intimated that she was really fond of him, he had given in, and never regretted it. She was a handsome, lively young woman, and it was nice that now there were always four to play dominoes, which was his favorite game.

It suddenly occurred to him that life in Pei-chow must be rather dull for his ladies. He decided that now New Year was approaching, he would try to select some nice presents for them.

He went to the door and called the clerk.

"Is none of my lieutenants back yet?" he asked.

"No, Your Honor," the clerk replied. "First they had a long consultation in the chancery with the Honorable Chu Ta-yuan, then they left all together."

"Tell the groom to bring my horse!" Judge Dee ordered. He

117

reflected that while his lieutenants were gathering material on the Lan murder, he had better go and see Pan Feng. On the way out there he would pass by Yeh Pin's paper shop, and inquire whether Yeh Tai had made his appearance yet. He could not get rid of the uneasy feeling that Yeh Tai's prolonged absence meant that new trouble was brewing.

Thirteenth Chapter: THE JUDGE CONVERSES WITH AN
ANTIQUE DEALER; HE IS TOLD THE EFFECT OF LACQUER
POISONING

JUDGE DEE halted his horse in front of the paper shop and called out to the clerk standing by the door that he wanted to see Yeh Pin.

The old paper merchant came hurriedly outside and respectfully invited the judge to come inside for a cup of tea. But Judge Dee did not descend from his horse; he said he only wanted to know whether Yeh Tai had come back.

"No, Your Honor," Yeh Pin said with a worried look, "he still hasn't turned up! I have sent my clerk around to the restaurants and gambling clubs he frequents, but nobody has seen him. I am really getting afraid that he has met with an accident."

"If he isn't back tonight," Judge Dee said, "I'll have placards put up with his description, and I'll warn the military police. I wouldn't worry, though. Your brother didn't impress me as a man who is an easy victim for footpads or other crooks. Let me know after the evening meal."

119

He spurred on his horse and rode to the street where Pan Feng lived. It struck him again how desolate that part of the city was. Even at this hour, when the time for the evening meal was drawing near, the street was completely deserted.

The judge descended in front of Pan's compound and fastened the reins of his horse to the iron ring in the wall. He had to knock on the door many times with the handle of his whip before Pan came to open it.

He looked very surprised when he saw the judge. Leading him to the hall he apologized profusely that there was no fire. He said:

"I'll bring here immediately the brazier from my workshop!"

"Don't bother," Judge Dee said, "we can have our talk there. I always like to see the rooms where people work."

"But it is in terrible disorder!" Pan cried out. "I had just begun sorting my things out!"

"Don't worry," the judge said curtly. "Lead the way."

Upon entering he saw that the small atelier was indeed looking more than ever like a lumber room. A number of larger and smaller porcelain vases stood about on the floor together with two packing cases, and the table was littered with books, boxes and packages. But the coal in the copper brazier was glowing and kept the small room well heated.

Pan helped the judge to take off his heavy fur coat, and made him sit down on the stool next to the brazier. While the curio-dealer scurried to the kitchen to prepare the tea, Judge Dee looked curiously at the heavy chopping knife that was lying on the table, on an oily rag. Evidently Pan had been busy cleaning it when the judge knocked on the door. His eyes fell on a larger square object standing by the side of the table, covered with a piece of wet cloth. He was just going to lift the cloth in idle curiosity when Pan entered.

"Don't touch it!" he called out.

As Judge Dee shot him an astonished look, Pan hurriedly explained:

"That is a small lacquer table I am repairing, Your Honor. Wet lacquer should not be touched with bare hands, it will cause a violent skin infection."

Judge Dee vaguely remembered having heard about the painful effects of lacquer poisoning. While Pan filled the cups, he said:

"That seems a beautiful cleaver you have there!"

Pan took the large knife up, and carefully felt the edge of the blade with his thumb.

"Yes," he said, "it's more than five hundred years old. It was used to kill the sacrificial oxen in the temple. But the blade is still perfect."

Judge Dee sipped his tea. He noticed how still it was in the house; he did not hear a sound.

"I regret," he said suddenly, "that I must ask you an awkward question. The man who murdered your wife knew beforehand that you were going to leave town. Your wife must have told him that. Do you have any indication that she had relations with another man?"

Pan Feng grew pale. He gave the judge an uneasy look.

"I must confess," he said unhappily, "that for the last few weeks I had been noticing a certain change in my wife's attitude to me. It's hard to put these things in words, but . . ."

He hesitated. When the judge made no comment he went on:

"I don't like to proffer wild accusations, but I can't help thinking that Yeh Tai had something to do with it. He often came to see my wife when I was out. My wife was not an unattractive woman, Your Honor; sometimes I suspected that Yeh Tai was trying to persuade her to leave me, so that he could sell her to a wealthy man as a concubine. My wife liked luxury, and I could of course never give her any expensive presents, and . . ."

"Except for those golden bracelets set with rubies," Judge Dee remarked dryly.

"Golden bracelets?" Pan Feng exclaimed, astonished. "Your Honor must be mistaken! She had only one silver ring, which her aunt gave her."

The judge rose.

"Don't try to fool me, Pan Feng," he said sternly. "You know as well as I that your wife had two heavy golden bracelets and several hairpins of solid gold."

"Impossible, Your Honor!" Pan said excitedly. "She never had anything like that."

"Come along," Judge Dee said coldly, "I'll show them to you."

He went into the bedroom, Pan following on his heels. Pointing to the clothes boxes the judge ordered:

"Open the one on top, you'll find the jewels inside!"

When Pan had lifted the lid Judge Dee saw that the box was half-filled with an untidy pile of ladies' garments. He remembered clearly that the other day it had been packed with neatly folded clothes, and that Tao Gan had carefully replaced them after he had searched the box.

He watched intently while Pan took the clothes out and piled them up on the floor. When the box was empty Pan exclaimed with relief: "Your Honor sees that there are no jewels here!"

"Let me try," Judge Dee said, pushing Pan aside. Stooping over

122

the box he lifted the cover of the secret compartment in the bottom. It was empty.

Righting himself he remarked coldly:

"You are not a very clever man, Pan Feng. Hiding those jewels won't help you. Tell the truth!"

"I swear, Your Honor," Pan said earnestly, "that I never even knew about that secret compartment."

Judge Dee stood thinking a moment. Then he slowly surveyed the room. Suddenly he stepped up to the left window. He pulled at the iron bar that seemed to be bent. It came out in two pieces. Feeling the other bars he found that all had been sawn through, then carefully replaced in their original position.

"A burglar has been here during your absence," he said.

"But none of my money was missing when I came back from the tribunal," Pan Feng said, astonished.

"What about those clothes?" the judge asked. "When I examined this room, that box was full. Can you tell me what garments are missing?"

After he had rummaged through the crumpled-up clothes, Pan said:

"Yes, I don't see two rather valuable robes of heavy brocade with a sable lining that my wife got as a marriage present from her aunt."

Judge Dee nodded slowly. Looking around he said:

"There seems to be something else missing too. Let me see now . . . Of course. There was a small red-lacquered table standing in the corner over there."

"Oh yes," Pan said, "that is the one I am repairing now."

The judge stood very still, deep in thought. Letting his whiskers glide through his fingers he saw a pattern gradually emerging.

What a fool he had been not to see this earlier! The clue of the jewels had been there all the time. From the very beginning the criminal had made a big mistake. And he had failed to notice it! But now everything fell into its place.

At last the judge roused himself from his thoughts. He said to Pan Feng, who had been watching him anxiously:

"I believe you are speaking the truth, Pan Feng. Let's go back to the other room."

While Judge Dee slowly drank a cup of tea, Pan Feng put on a pair of gloves and lifted the wet cloth.

"This is the red table Your Honor spoke about," he said. "It's quite a good old piece, but I had to put on a new coat of lacquer. The other day, before leaving for Five Rams Village, I had put it in the corner of the bedroom to dry. Unfortunately somebody must have touched it afterward, for when I inspected it this morning I found a large smudge on the top. I am now repairing that corner."

Judge Dee put his cup down. He asked:

"Could your wife have touched it?"

"She knew better than that, Your Honor!" Pan replied with a smile. "I have warned her often enough about lacquer poisoning, she knew how painful it is! Last month Mrs. Loo of the cotton shop came to see me. She had a nasty case of it, her hand was swollen and covered with sores. She asked me how it should be treated. I told her . . . ."

"How do you know that woman?" Judge Dee interrupted.

"When she was still a child," Pan said, "her parents lived next door to my former house, over in the west city. After she had married I lost sight of her. Not that I minded much, for I never cared for the women in that family. Her father was a decent

124

merchant, but her mother was of Tartar descent and dabbled in black magic. Her daughter had the same weird interests, she was always preparing strange potions in the kitchen, and sometimes would fall into a trance, and then say gruesome things. Apparently she knew my new address, and so came to consult me about her poisoned hand. She also told me then that her husband was dead."

"That is very interesting indeed," the judge said. He gave Pan a pitying look, then added: "I now know who committed this foul crime, Pan Feng. But the criminal is a dangerous maniac, and such people have to be handled with great care. Stay at home tonight and nail boards over that window in the bedroom. And keep your front door locked. Tomorrow you'll know."

Pan Feng had been listening dumbfounded. Judge Dee did not give him time to ask questions. He thanked Pan for the tea and left.

125

Fourteenth Chapter: A YOUNG WIDOW IS HEARD IN
THE TRIBUNAL; SHE IS PUNISHED FOR CONTEMPT OF COURT

WHEN Judge Dee came back to the tribunal he found Ma Joong, Chiao Tai and Tao Gan waiting for him in his private office. One look at their drawn faces sufficed to show that they had no good news.

"Mr. Chu Ta-yuan had drawn up an excellent plan," Ma Joong reported disconsolately, "but we failed to discover any further clues. Chu Ta-yuan together with Chiao Tai went the round of all the notables, and made a list of all the pupils Master Lan ever had. Here it is, but it doesn't look very promising." He pulled a paper roll from his sleeve and presented it to Judge Dee. While the judge scanned it, Ma Joong pursued: "I myself went with Tao Gan and Sergeant Hoong to search Master Lan's house. All in vain; we found nothing that even suggested that Lan ever had trouble with anybody. Then we questioned the master's chief assistant, a nice young fellow called Mei Cheng. He told us something that might be important."

126

Up to now the judge had not been listening very carefully, his mind was on the startling discoveries he had made in Pan's house. But now he sat up and asked eagerly:

"What was that?"

"He said," Ma Joong continued, "that once when he came back to the master's house unexpectedly at night, he heard him talking to a woman."

"Who was the woman?" Judge Dee asked tensely.

Ma Joong shrugged his shoulders. He said:

"Mei Cheng did not see her, he only heard through the door a few indistinct words that did not seem to make any sense. He did not recognize the woman's voice, but he did notice that she seemed angry. Mei Cheng is a straightforward, honest youngster, he wouldn't dream of eavesdropping, so he quickly left."

"But it proves at least that Master Lan did have some connection with a woman," Tao Gan said eagerly.

Judge Dee did not comment. He asked instead:

"Where is Sergeant Hoong?"

"When we were through in Master Lan's house," Ma Joong replied, "the Sergeant went to the market to question the two youngsters about the appearance of that Tartar fellow. He said he would be back here for dinner. Chiao Tai had seen Chu Ta-yuan to his house earlier, and joined us later in Lan's house."

Three beats of the bronze gong resounded through the tribunal.

Judge Dee said with a frown:

"That is the evening session. I have summoned a Mrs. Loo, a widow whose husband died under suspect circumstances. I plan to let her go after a few routine questions, and I hope no other matters are brought up during the session. For I have to tell you that this afternoon I made an important discovery in Pan Feng's

127

house. It will probably solve the sordid crime committed there."

His three lieutenants stormed him with questions, but the judge raised his hand.

"After the session when Hoong is back also," he said, "I shall explain to you my theory."

He rose and with the assistance of Tao Gan quickly donned his official robes.

Judge Dee saw that again a large number of people had assembled in the court hall; all were eager to hear the latest news about the murder of Lan Tao-kuei.

When the judge had opened the session, he first announced that the investigation of the poisoning of the boxing champion had made good progress. He said that the tribunal was now in the possession of some important clues.

Then he filled out a slip for the warden of the jail. A hubbub of voices arose from the audience as they saw Mrs. Kuo bringing in the widow Loo. The headman led her before the bench, and Mrs. Kuo withdrew.

Judge Dee noticed that Mrs. Loo had spent great care on her appearance. Her face was made up with a discreet application of rouge, and her eyebrows were carefully penciled. Clad in a simple, dark-brown padded robe, she made a striking figure, but the rouge could not conceal the cruel lines of her small mouth. Before kneeling on the stone flags she shot the judge a quick look, but she gave no indication of having recognized him.

"State your name and profession!" Judge Dee ordered.

"This insignificant person," Mrs. Loo replied in a measured voice, "is the widow Loo, nee Chen. She manages the cotton shop of her late husband, Loo Ming."

When these details had been duly recorded, the judge said:

"I intended to ask you for some elucidation of your husband's death, and therefore had you called for answering some simple questions. Since you refused to come voluntarily, I had to issue a warrant, and shall now question you here in the tribunal."

"The death of my husband," Mrs. Loo said coldly, "occurred before Your Honor had taken up office here, and it was duly registered by Your Honor's predecessor. This person fails to see on what grounds Your Honor intends to reopen this case. As far as this person knows, no accusation was brought against her in this tribunal."

Judge Dee reflected that this was a clever and eloquent woman. He said curtly:

"This tribunal deems it necessary to verify some remarks pertaining to your late husband's illness, made by the coroner of this court."

Suddenly Mrs. Loo rose. Half-turning to the audience, she shouted:

"Shall a hunchback be allowed to cast aspersions on an honorable widow? Everyone knows that a man deformed in body is also deformed in character."

Judge Dee rapped his gavel on the bench. He called out angrily:

"You shall not revile an officer of this court, woman!"

"What a court!" Mrs. Loo said with contempt. "Didn't you, the magistrate, the other night come in disguise to my house? And when I wouldn't let you in, didn't you send for me privately today, without a warrant or anything?"

The judge grew pale with anger. With an effort he took a hold on himself. He said in an even voice:

"This woman is guilty of contempt of court. She shall be given fifty lashes!"

A murmur rose from the crowd; it was evident that they did not agree. But the headman quickly stepped up to Mrs. Loo. He

A woman is punished for contempt of court

grabbed her by her hair, and forced her down on her knees. Two constables tore her robe and undergarment down to her waist, and two others on either side put a foot on her calves and tied her hands on her back. The headman let the light whip swish through the air.

After the first few lashes Mrs. Loo screamed:

"The dog official! Thus he vents his anger on a decent woman who scorned him! He . . ."

Her voice changed into wild screams as the whip cut into her bare back. But when the headman stopped to mark with a tally that ten strokes had been given, she called out:

"Our Master Lan is murdered, but that dog official thinks only of seducing a woman. He . . ."

The whip came down again, and she could only scream. When the headman paused for marking the twentieth stroke, she tried to speak but could not. After five more strokes she sank forward with her face on the floor.

At a sign from the judge the headman lifted her head and burned pungent incense under her nose till she regained consciousness. When at last she opened her eyes, she was too weak to sit up. The headman had to support her by the shoulders, while a constable held her head up by the hair.

Judge Dee said coldly:

"Mrs. Loo, you have offended this court and received half of the prescribed punishment. Tomorrow you shall be heard again. It shall depend on your own behavior whether the other half will be inflicted on you or not."

Mrs. Kuo appeared, and together with three constables they carried Mrs. Loo back to the jail.

Just when Judge Dee was about to raise his gavel for closing

131

the session, an old peasant came forward. He started upon a long story about his having accidentally bumped into a cake vendor carrying a tray with brittle cakes, on the corner of the street outside. The peasant spoke in the local dialect, and the judge had the greatest difficulty in following what he said. At last he understood what it was all about. The peasant was perfectly willing to compensate for the loss of fifty cakes, for that had been approximately the number that had been on the tray. But the vendor insisted that there had been a hundred, and wanted payment for that amount.

Then the vendor kneeled in front of the bench. His language was even harder to understand. He swore that there had been at least a hundred cakes, and accused the old peasant of being a crook and a liar.

The judge felt tired and nervous. With an effort he concentrated his mind on this quarrel. He told a constable to run outside and scoop up the broken cakes, and bring them to the tribunal together with one new cake from the street stall. He told the scribe to bring a pair of scales.

While they were gone Judge Dee leaned back in his chair, thinking again about the incredible insolence of Mrs. Loo. The only explanation was, of course, that there had been really something very wrong with her husband's death.

When the constable came back with the broken cakes, packed in a piece of oil paper, Judge Dee put the package on the scales. It weighed about 1,200 grams. Then he weighed the one new cake, and found it weighed about 20 grams.

"Give that lying vendor twenty strokes with the bamboo!" the judge said disgustedly to the headman.

Now there were some acclamations from the audience, they liked this quick and just decision.

When the vendor had received his punishment, Judge Dee closed the session.

In his private office the judge wiped the perspiration from his forehead. Pacing the floor he burst out:

"In my twelve years as a magistrate I have dealt with some nasty women, but never one like this! That foul insinuation about my visit!"

"Why didn't Your Honor immediately deny the charges of that evil woman?" Ma Joong asked indignantly.

"That would only have made it seem worse," Judge Dee said in a tired voice. "After all, I did go there at night, and in disguise. She is very clever, and she knows exactly how to get the sympathy of the crowd."

He angrily pulled his beard.

"In my opinion," Tao Gan observed, "she is not so clever. Her best policy would have been to answer quietly all questions, and refer to Dr. Kwang's certificate. She ought to have known that making all this trouble serves only to make us think that she really murdered her husband."

"She doesn't care a tinker's curse what we think!" Judge Dee said bitterly. "She is only out to prevent a second investigation of Loo Ming's death, because that will prove her guilt. And today she went a long way in reaching that object."

"We shall have to handle this affair with the greatest care," Chiao Tai remarked.

"We certainly shall!" Judge Dee said.

Suddenly the headman came rushing into the office.

"Your Honor," he said excitedly, "just now a shoemaker came to the tribunal with an urgent message from Sergeant Hoong!"

Fifteenth Chapter: SERGEANT HOONG VISITS THE COVERED MARKET; HE MEETS THE HOODED MAN IN A WINE HOUSE

STROLLING aimlessly from one street stall to another, Sergeant Hoong noticed that dusk was falling. He thought he had better go back to the tribunal.

His patient questioning of the two young men who had entered the bathhouse with the Tartar youth had produced very little result. They had not been able to add anything to the information given by their friend who had been interrogated by Judge Dee. The two had said that the Tartar had seemed to them just another young fellow; the only thing that had struck them had been the pallor of his face. They had not noticed the lock of hair and the Sergeant reflected that the first youngster might well have mistaken a slip of the scarf for it.

He stood looking for a moment at the shop of a pharmacist, and tried to identify the queerly shaped roots and dried small animals that lay in trays in front of the counter.

A large man brushed past him. The Sergeant turned around and saw a broad back, and a pointed black hood.

He quickly elbowed his way through a group of loiterers and was just in time to see the man disappear around the next corner.

He hurried after him, and saw him again, standing in front of a jeweler's counter. The hooded man asked something, and the jeweler took out a tray with glittering objects, which the man started to examine.

The Sergeant came as near as he dared, eager to catch a glimpse of the man's face. But the side of the hood prevented that. Hoong walked up to the noodle stall next to the jeweler's, and ordered a bowl. While the vendor was ladling out the noodles, the Sergeant kept his eyes on the hooded man. But now two other prospective buyers were talking to the jeweler, and obstructed the Sergeant's view. He saw only the gloved hands of the hooded man, who was examining a glass bowl filled with red stones. He pulled off one glove and picked up a ruby which he put in the palm of his right hand. He rubbed the stone with his forefinger. The two other buyers walked on, and now the Sergeant had a full view of the man. But he was standing with his head bent, and Sergeant Hoong still could not see his face.

The Sergeant was so excited that he could hardly swallow his noodles. He saw the jeweler raise his hands to heaven and start to talk volubly. Evidently he was discussing the price with the hooded man. But although the Sergeant strained his ears, he could not hear what was being said because of the confused talk of the noodle-eaters standing by his side.

He quickly took a mouthful. When he looked again the jeweler was shrugging his shoulders. He wrapped up something small in

135

a piece of paper and handed it to the hooded man, who turned around quickly and disappeared in the crowd.

Sergeant Hoong put his bowl, still half-full with noodles, down on the counter and went after him.

"Hey, grandpa, don't you like my noodles?" the vendor shouted indignantly. But the Sergeant did not hear him. He had spotted the hooded man just as he had entered a wine house.

The Sergeant heaved a sigh of relief. Halting in his steps he peered over the heads of the crowd. He deciphered with difficulty the half-effaced characters on the grimy signboard. It read: THE BREEZE OF SPRING.

He scrutinized the passers-by, looking for somebody he knew. But he saw only coolies and small merchants. Suddenly he recognized a bootmaker he sometimes patronized. He quickly grabbed him by his sleeve. The man opened his mouth for an angry question, but when he recognized the Sergeant his face lit up in a smile.

"How are you, Master Hoong?" he asked politely. "When shall this person have the honor of making a nice pair of good winter boots for you?"

Sergeant Hoong pulled him over to the side of the street. He took from his sleeve the small card case of faded brocade he kept his visiting cards in, and one silver piece.

"Listen," he whispered, "I want you to run to the tribunal as fast as you can, and demand to see His Excellency the Magistrate. Tell the guards you have an urgent message from me, and show this card case as proof. When you see the judge, tell him to come immediately to that wine house over there, with his three lieutenants, to arrest a man we were looking for. Here, take this silver piece for your trouble!"

The shoemaker's eyes grew round as he looked at the silver

piece. He started to thank the Sergeant profusely, who quickly cut him short.

"Get on!" he urged. "Run as fast as you can!"

Then Hoong walked over to the wine house and went inside.

The room was larger than he had expected, more than fifty people were sitting in groups of three and four at the deal tables, drinking cheap liquor and talking noisily. A surly waiter was rushing around, balancing a tray with wine jugs on his raised hand.

The Sergeant quickly surveyed the room through the reeking smoke of the oil lamps. He saw no one with a black hood.

As he picked his way among the tables, he suddenly saw that at the back of the restaurant there was a kind of nook, next to a narrow door. There was just place for one small table, and there the hooded man was sitting, with his back to the room.

With a sinking heart the Sergeant looked at the wine jug in front of the man, and the narrow door. He knew that in low-class establishments like this, one had to pay immediately for what one ordered. If the hooded man decided to leave, he could do so any time he wished. And he had to keep him in the wine house at all costs till the judge arrived.

The Sergeant walked over to the nook, and tapped the hooded man on his shoulder. He looked around with a start, and two rubies which he had been examining dropped to the floor.

Sergeant Hoong's face grew pale as he recognized the man.

"What might you be doing here?" he asked incredulously.

The man shot a quick look at the crowd. No one paid any attention to them. He put his finger to his lips.

"Sit down!" he whispered, "I'll tell you all about it!"

He pulled a stool around next to him, and made the Sergeant sit down.

"Now listen carefully!" the man said. He leaned over to the Sergeant. At the same time his right hand came out of his sleeve with a long, thin knife. He stuck it with lightning quickness deep into the Sergeant's breast.

Hoong's eyes opened wide, he wanted to cry out, but a stream of blood came from his mouth. He sank forward on the table, groaning and coughing.

The hooded man observed him impassively, at the same time watching the room. Nobody was looking in their direction.

The Sergeant's right hand was moving. With a twitching finger he wrote one character of a family name in the blood on the table top. Then his frame shook in convulsions, and he was still.

The hooded man disdainfully rubbed the character out. He wiped off his bloody fingers on Sergeant Hoong's shoulder. After another quick look at the crowd he rose, opened the back door and was gone.

When Judge Dee, followed by Ma Joong, Chiao Tai and Tao Gan, came running into the passage leading to the Breeze of Spring, they saw that a group of people had gathered under the lantern over the front door, talking excitedly.

Judge Dee's heart sank. Someone called out: "Here are the men from the tribunal to investigate the murder!"

The people hastily made way, and the judge ran inside, followed by his three lieutenants. He pushed the men standing in the farthest corner aside. Then he stood stock-still, looking down on the body of Sergeant Hoong, slumped over the table in a pool of blood.

The owner of the wine house wanted to say something, but when he saw the faces of the four men, he quickly drew back and motioned to the other people to go over with him to the other side of the room.

After a long time Judge Dee stooped and softly touched the dead man's shoulder. Then he carefully raised the gray head, loosened the robe and inspected the wound. He slowly let down the head again on the table. As he folded his arms in his sleeves, his three lieutenants quickly looked away. They saw tears moistening Judge Dee's cheeks.

Tao Gan was the first to recover from this fearful blow. He scrutinized the table top, then looked at the Sergeant's right hand. He remarked:

"I think the brave fellow tried to write something in his own blood. There is a curious smudge here."

"We are just nothing compared to him," Chiao Tai said fiercely. Ma Joong bit his lips till the blood trickled from his chin.

Tao Gan went down on his knees and searched the floor. When he rose he silently showed the judge the two rubies he had found.

Judge Dee nodded. He said in a strange, hoarse voice:

"I know about the rubies. But now it's too late." After a pause he added: "Ask the owner whether our Sergeant came here with a man wearing a black hood."

Ma Joong called the manager. The man swallowed several times, then stammered:

"We . . . we know nothing about this, Your Excellency! A man . . . a man with a black hood was sitting alone at this table. None of us knew him. The waiter says he ordered one jug of wine and paid for it. Sometime after that, this poor gentleman must have joined him. When the waiter discovered him, the other man had left."

139

"What did the man look like?" Ma Joong barked at him.

"The waiter saw only his eyes, Excellency! The man was coughing, he had drawn the ear flaps of his hood together over his mouth, and . . ."

"It doesn't matter," the judge interrupted in a toneless voice. The manager scurried away.

Judge Dee remained silent. None of his assistants dared to speak.

Suddenly the judge looked up. He fixed Ma Joong and Chiao Tai with his burning eyes. After a few moments' thought he said harshly to them:

"Listen carefully! Tomorrow at dawn you will ride to Five Rams Village. Take Chu Ta-yuan with you, he knows many short cuts. Go to the village inn, and ask for a full description of the man who met Pan Feng there when he was staying at that inn. Then come back straight to the tribunal here, together with Chu Ta-yuan. Have you got that?"

As his two lieutenants nodded, the judge added in a forlorn voice:

"Bring the body of the Sergeant to the tribunal."

He turned around and left without another word.

Sixteenth Chapter: THREE HORSEMEN RETURN FROM AN EARLY RIDE; A MISGUIDED WOMAN TELLS ABOUT HER FOLLY

THE next day, toward noon, three horsemen, their fur caps covered with snow, halted in front of the tribunal. They saw many people filing into the main gate.

Ma Joong said, astonished, to Chu Ta-yuan:

"It seems there is a session!"

"Let's hurry," Chiao Tai muttered.

Tao Gan came to meet them in the main courtyard.

"His Excellency had to convene a special session of the tribunal," he informed them. "Some important facts have come to light which need immediate attention."

"Let's go to the judge's private office and find out," Chu Ta-yuan said eagerly. "There may be news about the Sergeant's murder."

"The session is about to begin, sir," Tao Gan remarked, "the judge said he was not to be disturbed now."

"In that case," Chiao Tai said, "we'd better go straight on to the

141

court hall. If you come with us, Mr. Chu, we'll get you a place near the dais."

"The front row is good enough for me," Chu Ta-yuan replied, "but you can take me in by the back entrance, so that I won't have to elbow my way through the crowd. There seem to be quite a lot of people."

The three men entered the corridor, and went into the court hall by the door behind the dais used by the judge. Ma Joong and Chiao Tai went to stand by the side of the raised platform; Chu Ta-yuan walked on and stood himself in the first row of spectators, behind the constables.

A confused murmur of voices rose from the packed hall. All were eying expectantly Judge Dee's empty armchair behind the high bench.

Suddenly there was silence. The judge appeared on the dais. As he sat down Ma Joong and Chiao Tai noted that his face was even more haggard than the evening before.

Letting his gavel descend on the bench, the judge spoke:

"This special session of the tribunal of Pei-chow has been convened to deal with important new developments in the case of the murder in the house of the curio-dealer Pan Feng." Looking at the headman he ordered: "Bring the first exhibit!"

Ma Joong shot Chiao Tai a bewildered look.

The headman came back carrying a large package wrapped up in oil paper. He carefully put it down on the floor, then took a roll of oil paper from his sleeve and spread it out on one end of the bench. He took the package up and put it there.

Judge Dee leaned forward and quickly undid the top. A gasp rose from the audience as the wrappers dropped down. On the bench stood the head of a snowman. The eyes were represented by two glowing red stones that seemed to look at the audience with a malevolent glare.

The judge said nothing. He looked fixedly at Chu Ta-yuan.

Chu slowly came forward, step by step, his eyes on the head. At a peremptory sign from the judge the constables quickly drew aside. Chu walked up to the bench till he stood directly below the head. He stared up at it with a strange, vacuous stare.

Suddenly he said in a queer, petulant voice:

"Give me back my red stones!"

As he raised his gloved hands, Judge Dee's hand shot out. He tapped with his gavel the top of the head, and the snow crumbled away. The severed head of a woman stood on the bench. The face was half-covered by the wet hair locks.

Ma Joong uttered a fearful curse. He made to jump down from the raised platform to throw himself on Chu Ta-yuan, but the judge clutched his arm in an iron grip.

"Stay where you are!" he warned him. Chiao Tai sprang to Ma Joong's side and held him back.

Chu Ta-yuan stood stock-still, looking at the woman's head with a dazed expression. Dead silence reigned in the hall.

Slowly Chu averted his gaze and looked down. Suddenly he stooped and picked up the two rubies that had dropped down with the snow. He took off his gloves and placing the stones in the palm of his left hand, swollen and covered with blisters, he rubbed them with the forefinger of his right. A childish smile spread over his broad face.

"Beautiful stones!" he whispered. "Beautiful red stones, like drops of blood!"

All eyes were on that uncanny, hulking figure, smiling happily like a child over its toys. No one noticed the tall veiled woman

143

whom Tao Gan led before the bench. As she stood facing Chu Ta-yuan, Judge Dee suddenly asked:

"Do you recognize the severed head of Miss Liao Lien-fang?"

At the same time Tao Gan ripped down the veil from the woman's face.

Chu seemed suddenly to wake up from a dream. His eyes darted from the face of the woman opposite him to the head on the bench. Then he said to the woman with a sly smile:

"We must quickly cover it up with snow!"

He fell on his knees and groped over the stone flags.

A murmur rose from the crowd, quickly increasing in volume. But it stopped when the judge imperiously raised his hand.

"Where is Yeh Tai?" he asked Chu.

"Yeh Tai?" Chu asked, raising his head. Then he burst out in loud laughter. "Also in the snow!" he shouted, "also in the snow!"

Suddenly his face fell, he looked frightened. With a quick glance at the woman he cried out in a plaintive voice:

"You must help me! I need more snow!"

The woman shrank back against the bench. She put her face in her hands.

"More snow!" Chu Ta-yuan suddenly shrieked. He frantically groped over the stone floor, tearing his nails in the grooves between the flagstones.

Judge Dee gave a sign to the headman. Two constables grabbed Chu's arms and pulled him up. He fought back wildly, shouting and cursing, foam bubbling from his mouth. Four other constables sprang forward, and with great difficulty the raving man was put in chains and led away.

Judge Dee announced gravely:

"This court accuses the landowner Chu Ta-yuan of having murdered Miss Liao Lien-fang, and suspects him of the murder of Yeh Tai. Mrs. Pan was his accomplice."

Stopping the angry voices from the audience with his raised hand, he continued:

"This morning I searched the residence of Chu Ta-yuan, and found Mrs. Pan living alone in one of the secluded courtyards. The head of Miss Liao was found in a snowman, in one of the back gardens. The exhibit before you now is a wooden dummy."

Then Judge Dee addressed the woman, saying:

"Mrs. Pan, nee Yeh, shall now truthfully state her relations with the accused Chu Ta-yuan, and describe how the said Chu Ta-yuan abducted and subsequently murdered Miss Liao Lien-fang.

"This tribunal has clear proof of Mrs. Pan's complicity in these crimes, and shall propose the death penalty for her. But a full confession may result in this court recommending the death penalty in one of its milder forms."

Slowly the woman raised her head. She began in a low voice:

"This person first met Chu Ta-yuan about one month ago, in front of a jeweler's counter in the covered market. He bought a golden bracelet set with rubies, and he must have noticed my envious glance. For, when later I was purchasing a comb from a vendor farther down the passage, I suddenly found him standing by my side. He struck up a conversation, and when he heard who I was he said that he often bought antiques from my husband. I felt flattered by his interest in me, and when he asked whether he could come and see me I soon agreed, and mentioned an afternoon when my husband would be away. He quickly put the bracelet in my sleeve, and went away."

Mrs. Pan fell silent. After some hesitation she went on with bent head:

145

"That afternoon I had put on my best robe, heated the oven-bed and prepared a jug of warm wine. Chu came and spoke very kindly to me, treating me as his equal. He quickly drank the wine, but he did not make any of the suggestions I was expecting. When I took off my robe, he suddenly became ill at ease, and when I slipped out of my undergarments he turned his face away. He told me curtly to put on my dress again, then continued in a kinder voice that he found me very beautiful and would like very much to make me his mistress. But I would have to prove that I could be trusted by doing him a service. I readily agreed for I wanted very much a liaison with this wealthy man who would certainly reward me liberally. I hated the life I led in that lonely house, the little money I saved was always taken away by my brother Yeh Tai . . ."

Her voice trailed off. On a sign of the judge the headman offered her a cup of bitter tea. She greedily drank it, then went on:

"Chu told me there was a girl who used to visit the covered market on certain days, together with an old woman. I was to go with him there, he would point out the girl to me, and I was to lure her away without the old woman noticing it. He indicated a day and a meeting place, gave me another golden bracelet and left.

"I met Chu on the appointed day, and he followed me, his face partly covered by a black hood. I tried to approach the girl, but the old woman stayed close by her all the time, and I had to give up."

"Did you recognize the girl?" Judge Dee interrupted.

"No, Your Honor, I swear I didn't!" Mrs. Pan cried. "I supposed she was some famous courtesan. A few days later we tried again. The pair had strolled to the southern section of the market, they were looking at a Tartar with a performing bear. I stood myself next to the girl and whispered as Chu had instructed me: 'Mr. Yü wants to see you.' The girl followed me without another word.

"I took her to an empty house nearby that Chu had indicated; he followed close behind. The door was ajar, and Chu quickly pushed the girl inside. He told me he would see me later, and locked the door in my face.

"When I saw the placards I realized that Chu had abducted a girl of a well-known family. I hastened to his house with a faked message from my husband, and begged him to set the girl free. But he said he had already secretly removed her to a secluded courtyard in his own mansion, and that no one would ever know she was there. He gave me a sum of money, and promised that he would soon come to visit me again.

"Three days ago I met him in the market. He said that the girl made trouble, she tried to attract the attention of the other members of the household, and he did not get anywhere with her. Since my house was located in a lonely neighborhood, he wanted to take the girl there for a night. I replied that that very day my husband would be away for two days. Chu came that night after the evening meal, dragging the girl along disguised as a nun. I wanted to speak to the girl, but Chu pushed me to the door, and ordered me to go out and not come back before the second night watch."

Mrs. Pan passed her hand over her eyes. When she spoke again her voice sounded hoarse.

"When I came back I found Chu sitting in the hall, half-dazed. I anxiously asked him what had happened, and he told me incoherently that the girl was dead. I rushed to the bedroom and found that he had strangled her. Frantic with fear I ran back to Chu and told him I would call the warden. I didn't mind helping him in a love affair, but I certainly refused to become involved in a murder case.

"Suddenly Chu became very calm. He curtly said that I was already his accomplice and guilty of the death penalty. But he would perhaps be able to cover up the murder, and at the same time take me into his house as a concubine, without anybody ever suspecting it.

"He took me back with him to the bedroom and forced me to strip. He carefully examined my entire body, and when he saw that I had no scars or large birthmarks, he said that I was lucky and that everything would be all right. He took the silver ring from my finger and told me to put on the nun's cloak that was lying on the floor. I wanted to put on my undergarments first but he became very angry, threw the cloak over my shoulders and pushed me outside, ordering me to wait in the hall.

"I don't know how long I sat there, shivering with cold and fear. At last Chu came back, carrying two large bundles. 'I have taken the girl's severed head, and your clothes and shoes,' he said calmly. 'Now everybody will think the body is yours, and you shall be safe in my house as my cherished mistress!' 'You are crazy!' I cried out, 'that girl is a virgin!' He suddenly flew into a terrible rage, he started cursing, foam came on his lips. 'A virgin?' he hissed at me, 'I saw the lecherous slut together with my secretary, under my own roof!'

"Trembling with fury he put one of the bundles in my hands, and we left. He told me to lock the front door from outside. We went to his house, walking in the shadow of the city wall. I was so afraid that I didn't notice the cold. Chu opened a back door at

148

the rear of the house, placed one of the bundles under the shrubs in the corner of the garden, and led me through several dark corridors to a separate courtyard. He said I would find everything I wanted there and left.

"My rooms were luxuriously appointed, and an old deaf-and-dumb woman brought me excellent food. Chu came the next day. He seemed very preoccupied and only asked where I had put the jewels he had given me. I told him about the secret compartment in my clothes box, and he said he would get them for me. I asked him to bring also some of my favorite robes.

"But when he came the next day he said the jewels were gone, he gave me only the robes. I asked him to stay with me, but he said that he had hurt his hand, and would come another night. I did not see him again. This is the complete truth."

At a sign from the judge the senior scribe read out his record of Mrs. Pan's confession. She agreed listlessly that it was correct and affixed her thumb mark to the document.

Then Judge Dee said gravely:

"You have acted very foolishly, and you'll have to pay for it with your life. But since Chu Ta-yuan instigated you, and later forced you to go on helping him, I shall propose for you the death penalty in one of its milder forms."

The headman led the sobbing Mrs. Pan to the side door where Mrs. Kuo stood waiting to take her back to jail.

Judge Dee said:

"The coroner shall examine the criminal Chu Ta-yuan. In the course of the next days it will become apparent whether his mind is permanently deranged. Should he recover, I shall propose for him the death penalty in its most severe form, for as well as Miss Liao and presumably Yeh Tai, he also murdered the Sergeant of

149

this tribunal. We shall at once institute a search for Yeh Tai's body.

"This court wishes to express its sympathy with the cruel loss suffered by Guildmaster Liao. At the same time, however, the court is obliged to stress that when daughters have reached marriageable age, it is not only their father's duty to select at once a suitable husband, but also to see to it that the wedding takes place as soon as possible. The wise men of old who drew up the rules for us to live by did not do so without very good reasons. This admonition is also meant for all other householders present at this session.

"Pan Feng shall restore the coffin containing Liao Lien-fang's body to Guildmaster Liao, so that it can be buried together with the recovered head. As soon as the higher authorities have decided how the murderer shall be dealt with, blood money will be paid to Mr. Liao out of Chu Ta-yuan's estate.

"For the time being that estate shall be administered by the comptroller of this tribunal, assisted by the secretary Yü Kang."

The judge closed the session.

Seventeenth Chapter: JUDGE DEE EXPLAINS A
FIENDISH MURDER; HE LEARNS THE SECRET OF THE PAPER
CAT

WHEN they were back in the private office, Judge Dee said in a tired voice:

"Chu Ta-yuan had a double personality. Outwardly he was the jovial, athletic fellow whom you, Ma Joong and Chiao Tai, could not help liking. But the core was rotten, corrupted by his brooding over his one physical weakness."

He gave a sign to Tao Gan, who quickly filled his teacup. The judge drank it eagerly, then continued to Ma Joong and Chiao Tai:

"I had to have time to search his house, and I had to take him completely unawares, for the man is diabolically clever. Therefore I had to send you two with him on that faked errand to Five Rams Village. If the Sergeant had not been murdered, I would have told you all last night my theory about Chu's guilt. But after that I felt I could not ask you to try to behave in a natural manner to Sergeant Hoong's murderer. I know that I myself couldn't have done it!"

151

"If I had known," Ma Joong said fiercely, "I would have strangled that dog with my own hands!"

Judge Dee nodded. There was a long pause.

Then Tao Gan asked:

"When did Your Honor discover that the headless body was not that of Mrs. Pan?"

"I should have suspected that immediately!" the judge said bitterly. "For the body showed one striking inconsistency."

"What was that?" Tao Gan asked eagerly.

"The ring!" Judge Dee replied. "Yeh Pin stated during the autopsy that the ruby had been taken out of it. Since the murderer wanted that stone, why didn't he simply remove the ring as it was from the body?"

As Tao Gan clapped his hand to his forehead, the judge went on:

"That was the murderer's first mistake. But I not only failed to discover that inconsistency, I also overlooked another clue that suggested that the body wasn't that of Mrs. Pan; namely, that her shoes were missing."

Ma Joong nodded.

"It's hard to see," he said, "whether those loose robes and flimsy underthings the wenches wear on their bodies fit them or not, but with shoes it is a different matter!"

"Exactly," Judge Dee said. "The murderer knew that if he left Mrs. Pan's clothes without her shoes, we might start wondering about their absence. And if he left the shoes, we might discover that they didn't fit the body's feet. So he made the clever move of taking away everything, surmising that this would confuse us so much that we would overlook the significance of the missing shoes."

Heaving a sigh the judge continued:

"Unfortunately his surmise was quite correct. Then, however, he made his second mistake. That put me on the right track, and made me realize what I had overlooked before. He had a mania for rubies, and could not bear leaving them in Pan's house. Therefore he broke into the bedroom while Pan was in prison, and took them from the clothes box. He also foolishly acceded to Mrs. Pan's request to take some of her favorite robes. But this fact made me realize that Mrs. Pan must be alive. For if the murderer had known about the hiding place when he committed the crime, he would have taken the stones then. Someone must have told him afterward, and that could only have been Mrs. Pan.

"Then the significance of the ring without the stone dawned on me, and I also understood why the murderer had removed all the clothes. It was to prevent us from discovering that the body was not that of Mrs. Pan. The murderer knew that the only person who could have discovered that was her husband, and he surmised, again correctly, that by the time Pan Feng would have cleared himself, the body would have been encoffined already."

"When did Your Honor connect Chu Ta-yuan with the crime?" Chiao Tai asked.

"Only after my last talk with Pan Feng," Judge Dee answered. "I began by suspecting Yeh Tai. I asked myself who the murdered woman could be, and since Miss Liao was the only woman reported missing, I thought, of course, it must be she. The coroner stated that the body was not that of a virgin, but I knew from Yü Kang's confession that Miss Liao wasn't, either. Further, Yeh Tai had—as we then thought—abducted Miss Liao, and he was strong enough to have severed her head. I thought for a moment of the attractive theory that Yeh Tai had killed Miss Liao in a fit

153

of rage, and that his sister had helped him to cover up the murder, and then disappeared voluntarily. However, I soon discarded that theory."

"Why?" Tao Gan asked quickly. "It seems to me very sound. We knew that Yeh Tai and his sister were very close, and this would give Mrs. Pan the opportunity to leave her husband, whom she didn't care for."

The judge shook his head.

"Don't forget," he said, "the clue of the lacquer poisoning. From Pan Feng's statement I knew that only the murderer could inadvertently have touched that table, covered with a coat of wet lacquer. Mrs. Pan knew all about it, she would have taken good care not to touch that table. Yeh Tai did not have lacquer poisoning, and you can't do what the murderer did to his unfortunate victim with gloves on.

"The lacquer poisoning pointed at Chu Ta-yuan. For I remembered two occurrences, rather trivial in themselves, that now suddenly acquired special significance. In the first place, the lacquer poisoning offered an explanation for Chu's sudden decision to have a hunting dinner outside instead of an ordinary meal inside, in the hall. He had to wear gloves all the time to conceal his poisoned hand. Second, it explained Chu's bungling the chance of shooting the wolf when Ma Joong and Chiao Tai went out hunting with him on the morning after the murder. Chu Ta-yuan had a terrible night behind him, and his hand was hurting badly.

"Further, the murderer had to live near Pan, and possessed presumably a very large mansion. I knew that he must have left Pan's house together with a woman no one should see, and with a large bundle. He could not risk meeting the night watch or a military-

154

police patrol, for those people have the laudable habit of halting and questioning persons walking about in the night with large bundles. Now we know that Pan lives in a deserted street, and from there one can reach the rear of Chu's mansion by walking along the inside of the city wall, where there are only old go-downs."

"But just before reaching his mansion," Tao Gan remarked, "he would have to cross the main road near the east city gate."

"That was but a small risk," the judge said, "because the guards at the gate scrutinize only the people who pass through the gate, not those who pass by it inside the city.

"When I had thus hit on Chu Ta-yuan as the most likely suspect, I asked myself, of course, at once what could have been his motive. Then it suddenly dawned on me what must be wrong with Chu. A healthy, vigorous man who has no offspring although he has eight wives, suggests that he has a physical defect; and one that may sometimes have dangerous effects on a man's character. The mania for rubies proved by the removal of the stone from the ring, and the burgling of Pan's house to get the bracelets, added a significant touch to my picture of Chu: that of a man with a distorted mind. And it was a maniacal hatred for Miss Liao that made him murder her."

"How could you know that at the time, sir?" Tao Gan asked again.

"I first thought of jealousy," Judge Dee replied, "the jealousy of an elderly man for a young couple. But I discarded that at once, for Yü Kang and Miss Liao had been engaged to be married three years already, and Chu's violent hatred was very recent. Then I remembered a curious coincidence. Yü Kang reported to us that

155

Yeh Tai told him he had learned Yü's secret from the old maid-servant, when Yeh Tai stood talking with her in the corridor in front of Chu Ta-yuan's library. Then, Yü Kang also told us that thereafter he had tackled the maidservant about this affair, again in the corridor in front of Chu's library. It occurred to me that Chu might well have overheard both conversations. The first, during which the maid told Yeh Tai about the meeting in Yü Kang's bedroom, supplied the reason for Chu's hatred for Miss Liao: she had, under Chu's own roof, given a man the happiness that nature had denied Chu himself. I could imagine that Miss Liao became to Chu the symbol of his frustration, and that he felt that possessing her was the only means by which he could ever restore his manhood. The second conversation he overheard, the one between Yü Kang and the maidservant, revealed to him that Yeh Tai was a blackmailer. Chu knew how intimate Yeh Tai was with his sister; he feared that Mrs. Pan might have told her brother about their meetings, possibly even about the girl in the covered market. He decided he could not afford the risk of Yeh Tai finding out and blackmailing him for the rest of his life, and therefore he resolved that Yeh Tai must go. That fitted the facts nicely, for Yeh Tai disappeared on the very afternoon of the day Yü Kang spoke with the old maidservant.

"When I had thus established that Chu Ta-yuan had both the motive and the opportunity for committing the crime, also another thought struck me. All of you know that I am not a superstitious man, but that doesn't mean that I deny the possibility of supernatural phenomena. When on the night of the feast in Chu Ta-yuan's house I saw a snowman sitting in a back garden, I clearly felt the sinister, evil atmosphere of violent death. I now remembered that, during the dinner, Chu had given me to understand that it was the children of his servants who made those snowmen. However, Ma Joong and Chiao Tai had told me that Chu also used to make those himself, to use as targets in his archery practice. It suddenly occurred to me that if one had to conceal quickly a severed human head in this freezing weather, it wouldn't be a bad solution to cover it with snow and use it as the head of a snowman. A solution that would especially appeal to Chu, because it further helped to assuage his abnormal hatred for Miss Liao. For it would have reminded him of his target practice, shooting arrow after arrow into the heads of the snowmen."

The judge fell silent, he shivered. He hastily pulled his fur mantle closer to his body. His three lieutenants stared at him with pale, haggard faces. The sinister atmosphere of that insane crime seemed to hover in the room.

After a long pause Judge Dee resumed:

"I was now convinced that Chu Ta-yuan was the murderer; I only lacked concrete proof. I had planned to explain to you my theory about Chu last night, after the session, and to discuss with you how to organize a surprise search of his mansion. If we did indeed find Mrs. Pan there, Chu was lost. However, Chu then murdered the Sergeant. If I had talked with Pan Feng half a day earlier, we would have proceeded against Chu before he could have killed Hoong. But Fate had decided otherwise."

A mournful silence fell in the room.

At last Judge Dee said:

"Tao Gan can tell you all the rest. After you two had left the city together with Chu, I went with Tao Gan and the headman to Chu's mansion, where we found Mrs. Pan. She was conveyed to the tribunal in a closed palanquin, without anybody knowing about it. Tao Gan has discovered in all bedrooms secret peep-holes, and my questioning of the old maidservant proved that she knew nothing about Yü Kang's affair. Now we know, indeed, from Mrs. Pan's confession that it was Chu himself who spied on Yü Kang and his fiancée. I presume that once Chu made some careless remark to Yeh Tai, and that the astute rascal guessed the rest. But when Yü Kang asked Yeh how he had come to know his secret, Yeh made up the story of the old maidservant, because he didn't dare to involve Chu in his blackmail scheme. Whether later Yeh Tai yet made bold to blackmail Chu, or whether Chu overheard Yü's talk with the maid and only feared that Yeh would try to blackmail him—as I surmised—these are things we'll probably never know. For Chu is insane, and I am convinced that Yeh Tai's dead body is lying somewhere out in the snow fields.

"I also talked with Chu's eight wives; what they told me about their life with Chu I wish to forget. I have already issued the necessary orders for them to be sent back to their respective families, and after the case has been closed they will receive a substantial portion of Chu's wealth.

"Chu Ta-yuan's madness places him beyond the pale of the law. A Higher Power shall judge him."

The judge took Hoong's old card case, that was lying on the desk before him. He softly rubbed his fingertips over the faded brocade, then he carefully put it away in the bosom of his robe.

He spread a sheet of paper out on the desk, and took up his writing brush. His three assistants hastily rose and took their leave.

Judge Dee first wrote a detailed report for the Prefect on the murder of Miss Liao Lien-fang, then he wrote two letters. One to Sergeant Hoong's eldest son, who was serving as steward in the house of Judge Dee's younger brother in Tai-yuan. The Sergeant had been a widower, his son was now the head of the family, and he would have to decide the place of burial.

The second letter was to his First Lady, at the address of her old mother, also in Tai-yuan. He began with a formal inquiry after the old lady's illness, then apprised his wife also of the Sergeant's demise. After the customary formal phrases he added a more personal note. "When someone who was very dear passes away," he wrote, "we lose not only him, but also a part of ourselves."

When he had handed the letters to the clerk for immediate dispatch, he ate his solitary noon meal, deep in melancholy thought.

The judge did not feel like thinking about Lan's murder or the case of Mrs. Loo; he felt utterly tired. He told the clerk to bring him the file with his notes on a plan for Government loans, to be issued without interest to farmers when the crops failed. This was his favorite project. He had worked on it with Sergeant Hoong many an evening, trying to formulate a proposal that would meet with the approval of the Board of Finance. Hoong had thought it could be done by economizing on other expenses of the district administration. When his lieutenants came in, they found the judge engrossed in calculations.

Pushing away the papers he said:

"We must have a consultation about the murder of Master Lan. I still think that it was a woman who poisoned him. But up to now the only indication we have of his knowing a woman well is the statement by that young boxer. He told you about a woman

159

visiting Master Lan at night, but said that the words he overheard gave no clue to her identity."

Ma Joong and Chiao Tai nodded ruefully.

"It only struck us," the latter said, "that neither used the customary greetings. We may conclude therefrom that they knew each other very well. But as you remarked before, sir, we knew that already because Lan didn't make any attempt to cover his nakedness when she entered his bath room."

"What were the exact fragments of conversation the youngster overheard?" Judge Dee asked.

"Oh," Ma Joong replied, "nothing special. She seemed to be angry because he avoided her, and Master Lan answered that it did not matter, and added a word that sounded like 'kitten.'"

The judge sat up abruptly.

"Kitten?" he asked incredulously.

He suddenly remembered the question of Mrs. Loo's small daughter. She had asked him where the kitten was her mother's visitor had been talking to. This changed everything! He said quickly to Ma Joong:

"Go at once on horseback to Pan Feng's house. Pan knew Mrs. Loo when she was still a child. Ask him whether she had a nickname!"

Ma Joong looked very astonished. But he was not in the habit of asking questions, and he immediately took his leave.

Judge Dee made no further comment. He told Tao Gan to prepare fresh tea, then discussed with Chiao Tai the solution of a difficulty that had arisen about the jurisdiction of the military police over the civilian population of the district.

Ma Joong came back in a remarkably short time.

"Well," he reported, "I found old Pan very depressed. The

news about his wife's misconduct has hit him harder than the first tidings about her having been murdered. I asked him about Mrs. Loo, and he said that her schoolmates used to call her by the nickname 'Kitten.' "

Judge Dee crashed his fist on the table.

"That's the clue I was hoping for!" he exclaimed.

Eighteenth Chapter: THE CORONER'S WIFE REPORTS ON TWO PRISONERS; A YOUNG WIDOW IS AGAIN HEARD IN THE TRIBUNAL

WHEN Judge Dee's three lieutenants had taken their leave, Mrs. Kuo came in.

The judge hastily motioned her to be seated and to pour herself a cup of tea. He felt very guilty toward this woman.

As she leaned forward over the desk to fill his cup first, Judge Dee again noticed the tinge of fragrance that seemed to be part of her.

"I came to report to Your Honor," she said, "that Mrs. Pan doesn't eat, and cries all the time. She asked me whether her husband could be allowed to see her once."

"That is against the rules," Judge Dee replied with a frown. "Besides, I don't think it would do either of them any good."

"The woman," Mrs. Kuo said softly, "realizes that she'll be executed, and she is resigned to her fate. But she now realizes also

162

that in many ways she did care for her husband, and she wants to apologize to him, so that she'll die with the feeling that she has atoned for at least part of her guilt."

The judge thought for a while. Then he said:

"The main purpose of the law is to restore the pattern, to repair as much as possible the damage caused by a crime. Since Mrs. Pan's apology may console her husband, her request shall be granted."

"I also report," Mrs. Kuo continued, "that I have treated Mrs. Loo's back with various ointments. The wounds will heal. At the same time . . ."

Her voice trailed off. As the judge nodded encouragingly, she pursued:

"She doesn't appear to be physically very strong, Your Honor, it's her remarkable will power that keeps her going. I fear that another whipping on her back might permanently impair her health."

"That's useful advice," Judge Dee said. "I'll remember that."

Mrs. Kuo bowed. After some hesitation she said:

"Since she doesn't say a word, I took the liberty of asking about her small daughter. She said that the neighbors were looking after her, and that anyway the tribunal would have to release her soon. I was thinking, however, of passing by Mrs. Loo's house and making sure. If the child isn't happy, I shall take her in our own house."

"Take her with you in any case!" Judge Dee said. "At the same time you might search Mrs. Loo's house and try to find a black Tartar dress, or some black garments that could be used as such. This is a thing that only a woman could decide!"

163

Mrs. Kuo bowed with a smile. The judge felt the impulse to ask her opinion about a possible liaison between Mrs. Loo and Master Lan but he quickly restrained himself. It was strange enough already that he consulted with a woman about the affairs of the tribunal. Instead he asked what her husband thought of Chu Ta-yuan's condition.

Mrs. Kuo slowly shook her small head.

"My husband," she said, "has again administered a strong soporific. He thinks that Chu's mind is permanently deranged."

Judge Dee sighed. He nodded and Mrs. Kuo took her leave.

When he had opened the evening session, Judge Dee first announced the rules regarding the jurisdiction of the military police, adding that they would be put up on placards throughout the district. Then he ordered the headman to lead Mrs. Loo before the bench.

The judge noticed that again she had spent much care on her person. She had done up her hair in a simple but striking way, and wore a new brocade jacket. She kept herself straight, although her shoulders evidently hurt her badly. Before kneeling she shot a quick look at the hall, and seemed disappointed that there were only a few spectators.

"Yesterday," Judge Dee said evenly, "you insulted this court. You are not a foolish woman, Mrs. Loo; I trust that this time you will answer my questions truthfully, in the interest of justice, and of yourself."

"This person is not in the habit of telling lies!" Mrs. Loo replied coldly.

"Tell me," the judge said, "whether it is true that next to your personal name, you also have the nickname Kitten?"

164

"Is Your Honor mocking me?" Mrs. Loo asked scornfully.

"It is the privilege of this court to formulate questions," Judge Dee said calmly. "Answer!"

Mrs. Loo wanted to shrug her shoulders, but suddenly her face twitched in pain. She swallowed, then replied:

"Yes, I do have that nickname. It was given to me by my late father."

Judge Dee nodded. He asked:

"Did your late husband occasionally use that form of address?"

An evil glint shone in Mrs. Loo's eyes.

"No!" she snapped.

"Do you," the judge continued, "occasionally wear the black dress worn by Tartar men?"

"I refuse to be insulted!" Mrs. Loo called out. "How can a decent woman wear a man's dress?"

"The fact is," Judge Dee observed, "that such a dress was found among your belongings."

He noticed that now for the first time Mrs. Loo seemed uneasy. After some hesitation she answered:

"Your Honor may be aware of the fact that I have Tartar relations. That dress was left in the house a long time ago, by a young cousin of mine from over the border."

"You will be conducted back to the jail," Judge Dee said, "and presently reappear here for further questioning."

When she had been led away, the judge read out two official announcements regarding a change in the laws on inheritance. He noticed that now the court hall was full, and that more people were coming in. Some spectators must have spread the news that Mrs. Loo was being heard again.

The headman brought before the bench three full-grown boys. They were very ill at ease, and shot apprehensive looks at the constables and the judge.

"You needn't be afraid!" Judge Dee said kindly. "You'll stand in the front row of the spectators, and look over a person who shall presently be led before this bench. Then you'll tell me if you have seen that person before, and if so, when and where."

Mrs. Kuo led Mrs. Loo in. She had dressed Mrs. Loo in the black dress she had discovered in her house.

Mrs. Loo walked with mincing steps toward the bench. With a dainty gesture she pulled the black jacket down, so that it revealed her small, firm breasts and her rounded hips. Half-turning to the audience, she adjusted the black scarf wound around her head at a slight angle. She smiled coyly and nervously plucked with her fingers at the lower rim of her jacket. Judge Dee reflected that she was a consummate actress. He gave a sign to the headman, who led the three youngsters in front of the bench.

"Do you recognize this person?" Judge Dee asked the eldest.

The boy looked with undisguised admiration at Mrs. Loo. She shot him a shy, sidelong glance, then a blush colored her cheeks.

"No, Your Honor," the youngster stammered.

"Isn't that the person you met in front of the bathhouse?" the judge asked patiently.

"It couldn't be, Your Honor!" the boy said with a smile. "That was a young man!"

Judge Dee looked at the others. They shook their heads, goggling at Mrs. Loo. She looked at them archly, then quickly covered her mouth with her hand.

The judge sighed. He gave a sign to the headman to lead the boys away.

As soon as they had left, Mrs. Loo's face changed as if by magic. It showed its former cold, malevolent expression.

"May this person inquire the meaning of this masquerade?" she asked with a sneer. "Must a woman whose back has been beaten raw now be insulted by dressing her up in a man's dress, and thus exposing her in public?"

Nineteenth Chapter: A MALICIOUS WOMAN REVILES THE MAGISTRATE; THE SUDDEN TRANSFORMATION OF A PAPER CAT

THE identification had failed, but Mrs. Loo's elaborate act had now firmly convinced Judge Dee of her guilt.

Leaning forward he said sternly:

"Tell this court about your relations with the late boxing master Lan Tao-kuei!"

Mrs. Loo righted herself. She shouted:

"You can torture and insult me as much as you like, it doesn't matter what happens to me. But I refuse to take part in foul slander that sullies the precious memory of Master Lan Tao-kuei, our national hero, and the pride of this district!"

Loud acclamations rose from the crowd.

The judge crashed his gavel on the bench. "Silence!" he shouted. Then he barked at Mrs. Loo:

"Answer my question, woman!"

"I refuse!" Mrs. Loo called out loudly. "You can torture me as much as you like, but you shall not drag Master Lan into your evil schemes!"

With difficulty Judge Dee mastered his anger. He said curtly: "This is contempt of court." Remembering Mrs. Kuo's warning, he reflected that he had to be careful in having legal severities applied to Mrs. Loo. He ordered the headman:

"Give this woman twenty strokes with the rattan across her hips!"

An angry murmur filled the hall. Someone cried: "Better catch Lan's murderer!" Others shouted "Shame!"

"Silence and order!" Judge Dee called out in a stentorian voice. "This court shall presently bring forward irrefutable proof that Master Lan himself accused this woman!"

The audience grew still. Suddenly the screams of Mrs. Loo resounded through the hall.

The constables had laid her face downward on the floor and pulled down the trousers of her Tartar dress. The headman immediately covered her hips with a piece of wet cloth, for the law was that a woman might be shamefully exposed only on the execution ground. While two of his assistants held her hands and feet, the headman let the rattan descend on her hips.

Mrs. Loo shrieked wildly, writhing on the floor. After the tenth stroke, Judge Dee gave a sign to the headman, and he stopped.

"You will now answer my question," the judge said coldly.

Mrs. Loo lifted her head, but she could not speak. At last she brought out:

"Never!"

Judge Dee shrugged his shoulders, and again the rattan swished through the air. Suddenly Mrs. Loo was still. The headman stopped and the constable turned her over on her back. They started trying to revive her.

Judge Dee barked at the headman:

"Bring the second witness before me!"

A sturdy young man was led before the bench. His head was shaved close, and he wore a simple brown robe. He had a pleasant, honest face.

"State your name and profession!" the judge ordered.

"This person," the youngster replied respectfully, "is called Mei Cheng. I have been Master Lan's assistant for more than four years and I am a boxer of the seventh grade."

The judge nodded.

"Tell me, Mei Cheng," he said, "what you saw and heard a certain evening about three weeks ago."

"As usual," the boxer replied, "this person took leave of the master after the evening exercises. When I was about to enter my front door, I suddenly remembered that I had left the iron ball in the training hall. I went back to fetch it, for I needed it for my morning exercise. Just as I was entering the front courtyard, I saw the master close the door behind a visitor. I only saw vaguely a black dress. Since I was familiar with all the master's friends, I knew I would not intrude and walked on to the door. Then I heard a woman's voice."

"What did the woman say?" Judge Dee asked.

"I couldn't distinguish any words clearly through the door, Your Honor," the boxer replied, "and the voice was completely unfamiliar to me. But she sounded angry, about his not coming to see her or so. When the master answered I clearly heard him saying something about a kitten. I knew that this affair was none of my concern, and I quickly left."

When the judge nodded, the scribe read out his record of what Mei Cheng had said. After the boxer had impressed his thumb mark on the document, Judge Dee told him he could go.

In the meantime Mrs. Loo had regained consciousness, and was kneeling again, supported by two constables.

Judge Dee rapped his gavel. He said:

"It is the contention of this court that the woman who visited Master Lan at night was Mrs. Loo. Somehow or other she had wormed herself into Master Lan's confidence, and he trusted her. Then she solicited his favors, but he would, of course, have none of her. In spiteful revenge she murdered him by dropping a jasmine flower containing a deadly poison into his teacup, when he was resting after his bath. She had entered the bathhouse disguised as a young Tartar. It is true that a few moments ago three witnesses failed to recognize her, but she is a good actress. When posing as the Tartar she imitated a man's behavior, while just now she deliberately stressed her womanly charms. However, this point is irrelevant. For I shall demonstrate now how Master Lan himself left a clue that directly points to this depraved woman."

There were some astonished exclamations from the spectators. Judge Dee felt that the atmosphere in the court hall was changing in his favor. The testimony of the straightforward young boxer had made a good impression on the crowd. He gave a sign to Tao Gan.

Tao Gan brought the square blackboard he had made on Judge Dee's instructions, just before the session. Six pieces of the Seven Board, made of white cardboard, had been pinned onto it. Each measured more than two feet across so that the spectators could clearly see them. Tao Gan set the board up on the platform, against the table of the scribe.

"Here you see," Judge Dee resumed, "the six pieces of the Seven Board, as they were found on the table in Master Lan's room." The judge held up a triangle of cardboard, and continued: "The seventh piece, this triangle, was discovered clutched in the dead man's right hand.

"The fearful effects of the cruel poison swelled his tongue, he could not call out. Therefore, with a last effort, he tried to indicate the criminal's identity by means of the Seven Board he was playing with before he drank the fatal cup.

"Unfortunately the convulsions started before he could complete the figure. And when he slid to the floor in his death struggle, his arm must have brushed the pieces and displaced three of them. But by slightly adjusting those three, and by adding the triangle found in his hand, the figure intended can be reconstructed beyond reasonable doubt."

Judge Dee rose. He took three pieces off and pinned them on again in a slightly different position. As he added the fourth piece and completed the figure of the cat, a gasp rose from the audience.

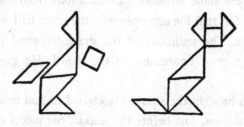

"With this figure," the judge concluded as he resumed his seat, "Master Lan designated Mrs. Loo as the murderess."

Suddenly Mrs. Loo shouted: "It's a lie!"

Shaking off the hands of the constables, she crawled toward the dais on hands and feet. Her face was distorted with pain. With a superhuman effort she dragged herself up on the platform, and crouched moaning against the side of the bench. She panted heavily, then clutched the edge of the board with her left hand. Trembling violently she changed the position of the three pieces Judge Dee had pinned on. Then she looked around at the audience, holding the fourth piece against her bosom. She cried hoarsely:

"Look! It's a hoax!"

Groaning she raised herself on her knees, and pinned on the triangle at the top of the figure.

Then she screamed:

"Master Lan made a bird! He never tried to leave . . . a clue."

Suddenly her face turned a deadly pallor. She fell all of a heap on the floor.

"That woman can't be human!" Ma Joong exclaimed when they were gathered in Judge Dee's private office.

"She hates me," the judge said, "because she hates all I stand for. She is an evil woman. Yet I must say I admire her fierce will power and her quick mind. That was no mean achievement to see at a glance how the cat could be changed into a bird—and that while she was half-dazed by pain!"

"She had to be an extraordinary woman," Chiao Tai observed.

"Else Master Lan would never have taken any notice of her."

"In the meantime," Judge Dee said worriedly, "she has maneuvered us into an extremely awkward position. We can't press the charge of Lan's murder; we must prove now that her husband died a violent death, and that she was concerned in it. Call the coroner."

When Tao Gan came back with the hunchback, Judge Dee said to him:

"The other day you said, Kuo, that you were puzzled by the bulging eyes of Loo Ming's corpse. You stated that a heavy blow on the back of the head may cause this phenomenon. But even if we assume that Dr. Kwang was in the plot, wouldn't Loo Ming's brother or the undertaker who dressed the body have noticed such a wound?"

Kuo shook his head.

"No, Your Honor," he replied, "there wouldn't have been any blood if the blow was inflicted by, for instance, a heavy mallet wrapped up in a piece of thick cloth."

Judge Dee nodded.

"An autopsy would, of course, show the crushed skull," he remarked. "But suppose this theory is incorrect, what other proof of violence could you find on the body? It all happened five months ago already!"

"Much depends," the hunchback answered, "on the kind of coffin used and conditions existing inside the tomb. But even if decomposition were far advanced, I think I could still trace poison, for example, by studying the condition of the skin and of the marrow inside the bones."

The judge thought for a while. Then he said:

"According to the law, exhuming a corpse without valid reason is a capital offense. If the autopsy failed to produce irrefutable proof that Loo Ming was murdered, I would have to tender my resignation, and place myself at the disposal of the authorities, to be judged for desecrating a grave. If one adds thereto the charge of having falsely accused Mrs. Loo of having murdered her husband, there is not the slightest doubt that I would be executed. The entire Government is behind its officials, but only as long as they don't make mistakes. Our Imperial civil service is such a vast organization that there can be no margin of leniency toward offending officials, even if they acted in good faith."

Judge Dee rose and started pacing the floor. His three lieutenants were watching him anxiously. Suddenly he halted.

"We shall have the autopsy!" he said firmly. "I'll take the risk!"

Chiao Tai and Tao Gan looked doubtful. The latter remarked:

"That woman knew all kinds of dark secrets. What if she killed her husband by casting a spell on him? That wouldn't leave any trace on the body."

The judge shook his head impatiently.

"I do believe," he said, "that there are many things in this world which are beyond our understanding. But I refuse to believe that August Heaven would allow the forces of darkness to kill a human being by magic alone. Ma Joong, issue the necessary instructions to the headman. The autopsy on the body of Loo Ming will take place this afternoon, in the cemetery."

Twentieth Chapter: AN AUTOPSY IS CONDUCTED IN
THE CEMETERY; A VERY SICK MAN TELLS A STRANGE STORY

THE North Quarter of the city looked as if a migration of the population were in progress. The streets were crowded with people, all moving toward the North Gate.

When the palanquin of Judge Dee was carried through the gate, the crowd made way in sullen silence. But as soon as they saw the small, closed sedan chair in which Mrs. Loo was carried along, they burst out in loud cheers.

The long file of people went through the snow hills to the northwest part of the city, toward the plateau where the main graveyard was located. They followed the path winding among the larger and smaller grave mounds, and converged on the open grave in the center, where the constables had erected an open shed of reed mats.

As he descended from his palanquin the judge saw that the temporary tribunal had been set up as well as circumstances permitted. A high wooden table served as bench, and the senior scribe sat at a side table, blowing in his hands to keep them warm. In front of the open grave mound stood a large coffin, supported on trestles. The undertaker and his assistants stood by its side. Thick reed mats had been spread out over the snow in front, and Kuo was squatting there by a portable stove, vigorously fanning the fire.

About three hundred people stood in a wide circle all around. The judge sat down in the only chair behind the bench, and Ma Joong and Chiao Tai stood themselves on either side of him. Tao Gan had walked over to the coffin and was examining it curiously.

The bearers put down Mrs. Loo's sedan chair and the headman pulled the screen curtain open. He drew back with a gasp. They saw the still body of Mrs. Loo, slumped over the crossbar.

Muttering angrily the crowd drew closer.

"Have a look at that woman!" Judge Dee ordered Kuo. To his assistants he whispered: Heaven forbid that the woman has died on our hands."

Kuo carefully lifted Mrs. Loo's head. Suddenly her eyelids fluttered. She heaved a deep sigh. Kuo removed the crossbar, and assisted her as she staggered to the shed, supporting herself on a cane. When she saw the open grave mound, she shrank back and covered her face with her sleeve.

"Nothing but play-acting," Tao Gan muttered disgustedly.

"Yes," Judge Dee said worriedly, "but the crowd loves it."

He struck the table with his gavel. It sounded curiously weak in the cold, open air.

"We shall now," he announced in a loud voice, "proceed to the autopsy on the corpse of the late Loo Ming."

Suddenly Mrs. Loo looked up. Supporting herself on her stick she said slowly:

Mrs. Loo arrives at the cemetery

"Your Honor is the father and mother of us, the common people. This morning in the tribunal I spoke rashly, because as a poor young widow I had to defend my honor, and that of our Master Lan. But I received the just punishment for my unseemly conduct. Now I beg Your Honor on my knees to let the matter rest here, and not to desecrate the coffin of my poor dead husband."

She sank to her knees and knocked her forehead on the ground three times.

A murmur of approval rose from the onlookers. Here was a reasonable proposal for a compromise, a settlement so familiar to them in their daily lives.

The judge tapped on the bench.

"I, the magistrate," he said firmly, "should never have ordered this autopsy if I didn't have ample proof that Loo Ming was murdered. This woman has a clever tongue, but she shall not prevent me from executing my duties. Open the coffin!"

As the undertaker stepped forward, Mrs. Loo again rose. Half-turning to the crowd she shouted:

"How can you oppress your people like this? Is that your conception of being a magistrate? You maintain that I murdered my husband, but what evidence did you bring forward? Let me tell you that although you are the magistrate here, you are not omnipotent! They say that the doors of the higher authorities are always open for the persecuted and the oppressed. And remember, when a magistrate has been proved to have falsely accused an innocent person, the law shall mete out to the offender the same punishment he wanted to give the falsely accused! I may be a defenseless young widow, but I shall not rest until that judge's cap has been removed from your head!"

179

Loud shouts of "She's right! We won't have an autopsy!" rose from the crowd.

"Silence!" the judge called out. "If the corpse fails to show clear proof of murder, I shall gladly take the punishment to be meted out to that woman!"

As Mrs. Loo again made to speak, Judge Dee pointed to the coffin and continued quickly: "Since the proof is there, what are we waiting for?" As the crowd seemed to hesitate, he barked at the undertaker: "Proceed!"

The undertaker hammered his chisel under the lid, and his two helpers set to work on the other side of the coffin. Soon they had loosened the heavy lid, and lowered it to the ground. They covered their mouth and nose with their neckcloth, and took the body out of the coffin together with the thick mat on which it had rested inside. They put it down in front of the bench. Some of the onlookers who in their eagerness to miss nothing had come very near, now drew back hastily. The corpse presented a sickening sight.

Kuo placed two vases with burning incense sticks on either side of the dead body. Having covered his face with a veil of thin gauze, he replaced his thick gloves by thin leather ones. He looked up at the judge for the sign to begin.

Judge Dee filled in the official form, then said to the undertaker:

"Before we start the autopsy, I want your statement as to how you opened the grave."

"In accordance with Your Honor's instructions," the undertaker said respectfully, "this person and his two assistants opened the tomb after noon. They found the stone plate that closes the grave in exactly the same condition as when they put it there five months ago."

The judge nodded, and gave the sign to the coroner.

Kuo cleaned the corpse with a towel dipped in hot water, then examined it inch by inch. All watched his progress in tense silence.

When he had completed the front side, he rolled the corpse over and began examining the back of the skull. He probed its base with his forefinger, then went on to examine the back of the corpse. Judge Dee's face grew pale.

At last Kuo rose, and turned to the judge to report.

"Having now completed the examination of the outside of the body," he said, "I report that there are no signs that this man met with a violent death."

The onlookers began to shout, "The magistrate lied! Set the woman free!" But the people in the front row called out to those behind to be quiet, and listen to the end of the report.

"Therefore," Kuo continued, "this person now requests Your Honor's permission to proceed to the inside examination, so as to verify whether poison has been administered."

Before the judge could answer, Mrs. Loo screamed:

"Isn't this enough? Must the poor body be submitted to further indignities?"

"Let that official put the noose around his own neck, Mrs. Loo!" a man in the front row shouted. "We know you are innocent!"

Mrs. Loo wanted to scream something again, but Judge Dee had already given the sign to the coroner, and the onlookers shouted at Mrs. Loo to keep quiet.

Kuo worked on the body for a long time, probing with a lamella of polished silver, and carefully studying the ends of the bones that were sticking out of the decomposed body.

When he rose he gave the judge a puzzled look. It was very still in the packed graveyard now. After some hesitation Kuo said:

"I have to report also that the inside of the body doesn't show any marks that poison was administered. To the best of my knowledge this man died a natural death."

Mrs. Loo screamed something, but her voice was drowned in the angry shouts of the crowd. They surged forward toward the shed, and pushed the constables aside. Those in front shouted:

"Kill that dog official! He has desecrated a grave!"

Judge Dee left his seat and went to stand in front of the bench. Ma Joong and Chiao Tai sprang to his side, but he roughly pushed them away.

When the people in the front row saw the expression on Judge Dee's face, they involuntarily stepped back and fell silent. Those behind them stopped their shouting, to hear what was going on.

Folding his arms in his sleeves the judge called out in a stentorian voice:

"I have said that I would resign, and I shall do so! But not before I have verified one more point. I remind you that as long as I have not yet tendered my resignation, I am still the magistrate here. You can kill me if you like, but remember that you are then rebels, rising against the Imperial Government, and that you will suffer the consequences! Make up your minds; I am here!"

The crowd looked with awe at the impressive figure. They hesitated.

Judge Dee went on quickly:

"If there are any guildmasters here, let them come forward, so that I can entrust to them the reburial of the corpse."

As a burly man, the master of the Butchers' Guild, detached himself from the crowd, the judge ordered:

"You will supervise the undertakers when they place the body

182

in the coffin, and you will see to it that it is replaced in the tomb. Then you will have the entrance sealed."

He turned around and ascended his palanquin.

Late that night a doleful silence reigned in Judge Dee's private office. The judge sat behind his desk, his shaggy eyebrows knit in a deep frown. The glowing coals in the brazier had turned to ashes, and it was bitterly cold in the large room. But neither the judge nor his lieutenants noticed it.

When the large candle on the desk began to splutter, the judge spoke up at last:

"We have now reviewed all possible means for settling this case. And we are agreed that unless we discover new evidence, I am finished. We have to find the evidence, and we have to find it quickly."

Tao Gan lighted a new candle. The flickering light shone on their haggard faces.

A knock sounded on the door. The clerk came in and announced excitedly that Yeh Pin and Yeh Tai asked to speak to the judge.

Greatly astonished Judge Dee ordered him to bring them in.

Yeh Pin entered, supporting Yeh Tai on his arm. The latter's head and hands were heavily bandaged, his face had an unnatural green color, and he could hardly walk.

When with Ma Joong and Chiao Tai's help Yeh Tai had been made to sit down on the couch, Yeh Pin said:

"This afternoon, Your Honor, four peasants from outside the East Gate brought my brother home on a stretcher. They had found him by accident, lying unconscious behind a drift of snow.

He had a fearful wound on the back of his head, and his fingers were damaged by frostbite. But they looked after him well, and this morning he regained consciousness and told them who he was."

"What happened?" Judge Dee asked eagerly.

"The last I remember," Yeh Tai said in a weak voice, "is that two days ago when I was walking home for dinner, I suddenly received a crushing blow on the back of my head."

"It was Chu Ta-yuan who hit you, Yeh Tai," the judge said. "When did he tell you that Yü Kang and Miss Liao had met secretly in his house?"

"He never told me, Your Honor," Yeh Tai answered. "Once I was waiting outside Chu's library, and heard him talk loudly inside. I thought he was having a quarrel with someone, and put my ear to the door. I heard him raving about Yü Kang and Miss Liao making love under his own roof; he used the most obscene language. Then the steward came and knocked. Chu was suddenly silent, and when I was admitted inside, I saw that he was alone, and quite calm."

Turning to his lieutenants Judge Dee said:

"That clears up the last obscure point connected with the murder of Miss Liao." To Yeh Tai he continued: "Having thus accidentally obtained this knowledge, you blackmailed the unfortunate Yü Kang. But August Heaven has already severely punished you for that."

"My fingers are gone!" Yeh Tai cried out despondently.

The judge gave a sign to Yeh Pin. Together with Ma Joong and Chiao Tai they helped Yeh Tai to the door.

184

Twenty-first Chapter: A CAPTAIN ARRIVES WITH
AN URGENT LETTER; THE JUDGE REPORTS IN THE ANCES-
TRAL HALL

THE next morning Judge Dee went out for an early ride. But in
the streets the people shouted at him, and near the Drum Tower
a stone nearly hit him.

He rode to the old drill ground, and galloped around it a few
times. Back at the tribunal he reflected that he had better not
show himself outside till he could call a session of the tribunal
and announce a solution of the case of Mrs. Loo.

The next two days he passed dealing with matters connected
with the district administration. His three lieutenants went out
every day, searching frantically for new clues. But all their attempts
were in vain.

The only good news came on the second day, in the form of a
long letter from his First Lady. She wrote from Tai-yuan that
the crisis had been tided over, and that her old mother was now
well on her way to a complete recovery. They were planning to
return to Pei-chow in the near future. The judge reflected sadly

that unless he solved the case of Mrs. Loo, he would never see his family again.

Early in the morning of the third day, when Judge Dee was sitting in his office eating his breakfast, the clerk announced the arrival of a captain from the Generalissimo's headquarters, carrying a letter which he had to hand to the magistrate personally.

A tall man came in, clad in full armor covered with snow. He bowed and handed the judge a large sealed letter, saying stiffly:

"I am under orders to take the answer back with me."

The judge shot him a curious look. "Be seated," he said curtly and opened the letter.

It stated that the secret agents of the military police had reported unrest among the population of Pei-chow. There were also reports about military preparations among the barbarian hordes high up in the north, and the Generalissimo deemed it a military necessity that the area at the back of the Northern Army be at peace. It was intimated that if the Magistrate of Pei-chow would send a request for the stationing of a garrison in his district, it would be complied with at once. The letter was signed and sealed by the Commanding General of the Military Police, on behalf of the Generalissimo.

Judge Dee grew pale.

He quickly took up his brush and wrote a reply of four lines: "The Magistrate of Pei-chow appreciates the prompt communication but begs to report that he himself will take this morning the necessary steps for ensuring the immediate return of peace and order in his district."

He impressed the large red seal of the tribunal on the letter, and gave it to the captain, who accepted it with a bow and took his leave.

Judge Dee rose and called the clerk. He told him to take out his full ceremonial dress, and to call his three lieutenants.

Ma Joong, Chiao Tai and Tao Gan looked astonished when they saw the judge clad in his court dress and wearing the gold-lined velvet ceremonial cap.

Looking sadly at the faces of the three men who had become his trusted friends, the judge said:

"This situation can't go on. I have just received a veiled complaint from the Generalissimo's headquarters about the unrest among the population of this district. They propose to station troops here; my capacity for administering Pei-chow is being questioned. I shall require your presence as witnesses to a brief ceremony in my own house."

As he walked along the covered corridors that connected the chancery with his private quarters, Judge Dee reflected that this was the first time he had visited his own house since his family had left for Tai-yuan.

The judge took his lieutenants straight to his ancestral shrine at the back of the main hall. The chilly room was bare except for a large cupboard that reached up to the ceiling, and an altar table on the left.

Judge Dee lighted the sticks in the incense burner, then knelt in front of the cupboard. His three lieutenants knelt down near the entrance.

Rising, the judge reverently opened the high double doors of the cupboard. The shelves were crowded with small, vertical wooden tablets, each standing on a miniature pedestal of carved wood. Those were the soul tablets of Judge Dee's ancestors, each marked in golden letters with their posthumous name and rank, and the year, day and hour of their birth and death.

The judge knelt again, and touched the floor three times with his forehead. Then, with closed eyes, he concentrated his thoughts.

The last time the ancestral shrine had been opened was twenty years ago, in Tai-yuan, when his father had announced to the ancestors Judge Dee's marriage with his First Lady. He had been kneeling with his bride behind his father. He saw before him the thin, white-bearded figure with the dear, wrinkled face.

But now his father's face was cold and impersonal. The judge saw him standing at the entrance of an immense assembly hall, lined on left and right by a crowd of grave men, standing motionless, all eyes fixed on himself, kneeling there at his father's feet. Across the vast expanse of the floor, at the back of the hall, he saw faintly the long robe, shimmering with gold, of the Grand Ancestor, sitting there motionless on his high throne. He had lived eight centuries ago, not long after the Sage, Confucius.

Kneeling humbly before this solemn assembly, the judge felt at peace and relaxed, like a man who has finally come home after a long and arduous journey. He spoke in a clear voice:

"The unworthy descendant of the illustrious house of Dee, named Jen-djieh, eldest son of the late Councillor Dee Cheng-yuan, respectfully reports that having failed in his duties to the state and the people, he will today tender his resignation. At the same time he will accuse himself of two capital crimes, namely having desecrated a grave without sufficient reason, and having falsely accused a person of having committed a murder. He was sincere in purpose, but his slender capacities proved unequal to the task entrusted to him. Reporting these facts this person respectfully begs forgiveness."

As he fell silent the vast assembly slowly faded away before his mind's eye. The last he saw was his father calmly rearranging the folds of his long red robe, in the gesture so familiar to him.

The judge rose. Having bowed again three times, he closed the doors of the shrine.

He turned around and motioned the three men to follow him.

Back in his private office the judge said in a steady voice:

"I now want to be alone. I shall draw up the official letter of resignation. You'll come back here before noon, and have the text of my letter put up on placards throughout the city, so that the people will be at rest."

The three men bowed silently, then fell on their knees and touched the floor three times with their foreheads, to signify that nothing could change their allegiance, whatever might befall the judge.

When they had gone, Judge Dee wrote his letter to the Prefect, describing his failure in detail, and accusing himself of the two capital crimes. He added that there were no grounds for asking leniency.

Having signed and sealed the letter, he leaned back in his armchair with a deep sigh. This had been his last official act as magistrate of Pei-chow. In the afternoon, as soon as the text was promulgated, he would hand the seals of office temporarily to the senior scribe, who would administer the district until another official arrived to take over.

Sipping his tea Judge Dee found that now he could view his own coming trial dispassionately. The death sentence was certain; the only point in his favor was that once, when serving as magistrate of Poo-yang, he had been granted an Imperial Inscription. He fervently hoped that the Metropolitan Court in consideration thereof would refrain from confiscating all his property. His wives and children would of course be taken care of by his younger brother in Tai-yuan. But the judge reflected that it is sad to live on charity, even with one's own relatives.

He was glad that at least his First Lady's mother had recovered. She would be a great help to her daughter in the trying days that lay ahead.

Twenty-second Chapter: JUDGE DEE RECEIVES AN UNEXPECTED VISIT; HE DECIDES TO CONDUCT A SECOND AUTOPSY

JUDGE DEE rose and walked over to the brazier. As he was standing there warming his hands, he heard the door open behind him. Annoyed at the disturbance he turned around. Then he saw that Mrs. Kuo had come in.

He gave her a quick smile, and said kindly:

"I am very busy just now, Mrs. Kuo. If there is anything of importance, you can report to the senior scribe."

But Mrs. Kuo made no move to take her leave. She stood there silently, with downcast eyes. After a while she said in a very low voice:

"I heard that Your Honor is going to leave us. I wanted to thank Your Honor for all his consideration . . . toward my husband and me."

The judge turned around and stood facing the window. The glow of the snow outside shone through the paper window panes. With an effort he said:

"Thank you, Mrs. Kuo. I greatly appreciate the assistance you and your husband have given me during my term of office here."

He stood still, waiting to hear the door close.

Then he noticed the fragrance of dried herbs. He heard a soft voice behind him saying:

"I know it's hard for a man to gauge a woman's thoughts."

When the judge quickly turned around to her, she continued hurriedly:

"Women have secrets of their own that a man can never fathom. No wonder that Your Honor couldn't discover that of Mrs. Loo."

Judge Dee stepped to her side.

"Do you mean," he asked tensely, "that you have found a new clue?"

"No," Mrs. Kuo said with a sigh, "not a new clue. An old one . . . . but the only one that solves the murder of Loo Ming."

The judge gave her a penetrating look. He said hoarsely:

"Speak up, woman!"

Mrs. Kuo drew her cloak close around her. She seemed to shiver. Then she spoke in a voice that sounded very tired:

"Bent on the daily household chores, mending clothes that aren't worth mending any more, sewing the felt soles of our old shoes, our thoughts wander. Straining our eyes in the flickering light of the candle, we work on and on, and idly we wonder . . . whether this is all. The felt sole is hard, our fingers are sore. We take the long, thin nail, we take the wooden mallet, and hammer the holes in the sole, one by one . . ."

Looking intently at the slender figure as she stood there with bent head, the judge groped for some kind words to say. But she suddenly went on in the same weary, detached voice:

"We draw the needle in and out, in and out. And our sad thoughts go in and out—weird gray birds that flutter aimlessly around a deserted nest."

Mrs. Kuo lifted her head and looked at the judge. He was amazed at the gleam in her wide eyes. She said very slowly:

"Then, one night, the idea comes. She stops her sewing, she takes up the long nail, and looks at it . . . as if she had never seen it before. The faithful nail that saves her sore fingers, the faithful companion of so many lonely hours of sad thoughts."

"Do you mean to say . . ." Judge Dee exclaimed.

"Yes, I do," Mrs. Kuo replied in the same toneless voice. "Those nails have only a very small head. When driven in entirely with the mallet, that tiny point would never be discovered among the hair on top of the head. No one would ever know how she murdered him . . . and set herself free."

The judge fixed her with his burning stare.

"Woman," he exclaimed, "you have saved me! That must be the solution! It explains why she was so afraid of an autopsy, and why that autopsy produced no result!" A warm smile lighting up his haggard face he added softly: "How right you are! Only a woman could have known this."

Mrs. Kuo looked at him silently. The judge asked quickly:

"Why are you sad? I repeat, you must be right. This is the only solution."

Mrs. Kuo pulled the hood of her cloak up and drew it over her head. Looking at the judge with a soft smile she said:

"Yes, you'll find that it is the only solution."

She went to the door and left.

As Judge Dee stood looking at the closed door, his face suddenly grew pale. He remained standing there a long time. Then

193

he called the clerk, and ordered him to tell his three lieutenants to come to the office at once.

Ma Joong, Chiao Tai and Tao Gan entered listlessly. But their faces lit up in an incredulous smile when they saw the expression on Judge Dee's face.

He stood erect in front of his desk, his arms folded in his wide sleeves. He said with shining eyes:

"I am confident, my friends, that at the very last moment we shall uncover Mrs. Loo's crime! We shall have a second autopsy conducted on the corpse of Loo Ming."

Ma Joong looked in consternation at his two companions. But then he grinned broadly, and exclaimed:

"If Your Honor says so, it means that the case is solved! When shall we have the autopsy?"

"As soon as possible," Judge Dee said briskly. "This time we shan't proceed to the cemetery, we'll have the coffin brought here to the tribunal."

Chiao Tai nodded.

"Your Honor knows," he said, "that the people are in a dangerous mood. I agree that it's much easier to keep them in hand here than outside in the open."

Tao Gan still looked doubtful. He said slowly:

"When I told the clerk to prepare the sheets of paper for the placards, I could see by their looks that they understood. By now the news that Your Honor is going to resign will be all over the city. I fear that a riot will break out when they hear about the second autopsy."

"I am fully aware of that," Judge Dee said in a steady voice, "and I am prepared to take the risk. Tell Kuo to prepare everything for the autopsy in the court hall. Ma Joong and Chiao Tai

194

shall go and see the masters of the Butchers' Guild, and Guild-master Liao. Apprise them of my decision and ask them to accompany you to the cemetery, to witness the taking out of the coffin, and accompany it back to the tribunal. If everything is done quickly and quietly, we shall have the coffin here in the tribunal before the people are aware that anything is happening. And when the news spreads, I trust that in the beginning their curiosity will be stronger than their resentment against me, while the presence of the guildmasters, whom they trust, will further help to prevent them from committing rash deeds. Thus I hope nothing untoward will happen till I open the session here in the tribunal."

He gave his lieutenants a reassuring smile, and they quickly took their leave.

Then the smile froze on Judge Dee's face. It was only by a supreme effort that he had kept up his cheerful mien in front of his lieutenants. Now he walked to his desk, sat down and buried his face in his hands.

Twenty-third Chapter: THE TRIBUNAL PREPARES A
SPECIAL SESSION; A WOMAN TELLS AT LAST HER AMAZING
TALE

AT NOON Judge Dee did not partake of the rice and soup that the clerk had placed before him. He could only drink a cup of tea.

Kuo had reported that the coffin had been brought to the tribunal without any interference. But now a large crowd was assembling in front of the main gate, shouting angrily.

When Ma Joong and Chiao Tai came in they looked very worried.

"The people in the court hall are in an ugly mood, Your Honor," Ma Joong said gravely. "And in the street outside those who couldn't find a place in the hall are shouting curses and throwing stones against the gate."

"Let them!" Judge Dee said curtly.

Ma Joong gave Chiao Tai an appealing look. Chiao Tai said:

"Let me call the military police, Your Honor! They could throw a cordon around the tribunal and . . ."

The judge crashed his fist on the table.

"Am I not the magistrate here?" he barked at his lieutenants. "This is my district, these are my people. I don't want any outside help, I'll manage them alone!"

The two men did not say anything, they knew it was useless. But they feared that this time the judge was wrong.

The gong sounded three times.

Judge Dee rose and crossed the corridor to the court hall, followed by his two lieutenants.

As the judge entered the hall and sat down behind the bench he was greeted by an ominous silence.

The hall was packed to overflowing. The constables stood in their appointed places, looking uneasy. On the left the judge saw Loo Ming's coffin, with the undertaker and his assistants by its side. Mrs. Loo stood in front of the coffin, supporting herself on a stick. Tao Gan and Kuo stood next to the table of the scribe.

Judge Dee hit his gavel on the bench. He said:

"I declare the session open."

Mrs. Loo suddenly shouted:

"What right has a resigning magistrate to open a session?"

An angry murmur rose from the crowd.

"This session," Judge Dee announced, "is convened to prove that the cotton dealer Loo Ming was foully murdered. Undertaker, open the coffin!"

Mrs. Loo stepped on the corner of the platform. She screamed:

"Shall we allow this dog official to desecrate again my husband's corpse?"

The crowd surged forward. Shouts of "Down with that magistrate!" rose on all sides. Ma Joong and Chiao Tai laid their hands on the hilts of the swords they kept concealed in the folds of their robes. People in the front row pushed the constable aside.

An evil glint shone in the eyes of Mrs. Loo. This was her triumph. Her wild Tartar blood exulted at the impending violence and bloodshed. She raised her hand and the people halted, looking at that striking figure. Her breast heaving she began, pointing at the judge:

"This dog official, this . . ."

When she took a deep breath, Judge Dee suddenly said in a matter-of-fact voice:

"Think of your felt shoes, woman."

With a cry Mrs. Loo bent and looked. When she righted herself Judge Dee saw for the first time real fear in her eyes. The people in front quickly relayed this unexpected remark of the judge to those behind them. As Mrs. Loo took hold of herself and looked at the audience, groping for words, a confused babble of voices came from the crowd. "What did he say?" people at the back of the hall shouted impatiently. When Mrs. Loo started to speak, her voice was drowned in the hammer blows of the undertakers. With Tao Gan's help, the undertaker quickly placed the lid on the floor.

"You'll now see the answer!" Judge Dee called out in a stentorian voice.

"Don't believe him, he . . ." Mrs. Loo began. But she halted as she saw that the crowd had attention only for the body that was lifted out of the coffin and placed on the reed mat. She shrank back against the side of the bench, her eyes fixed on the gruesome human remains stretched out on the mat.

Judge Dee hit his gavel on the bench. He spoke loudly:

"The coroner shall now examine only the head of the corpse. He shall pay special attention to the crown of the skull, and look between the hairs."

198

As Kuo squatted down, deep silence reigned in the packed hall. One heard only the muffled sounds of the people shouting in the street outside.

Suddenly Kuo righted himself, his face livid. He said hoarsely:

"I report, Your Honor, that among the hair I found a small iron point. It seems to be the head of a nail."

Mrs. Loo took hold of herself.

"It's a plot!" she screamed. "The coffin has been tampered with!"

But curiosity now dominated the onlookers. A thickset butcher in the front row shouted:

"My guildmaster himself sealed the tomb. Hold your peace, woman, we want to see what that thing is!"

"Verify your statement!" the judge barked at Kuo.

The coroner took a pair of clippers from his sleeve. Mrs. Loo sprang over to him, but the headman grabbed her and held her back. While she was fighting like a wildcat, Kuo extracted a long nail from the skull. He held it up to the crowd, then deposited it on the bench in front of the judge.

Mrs. Loo's body went limp. When the headman released her, she staggered blindly to the table of the scribe and stood there with bent head, supporting herself on the table edge.

The spectators in the front row shouted what they had seen to those behind them. The people started talking noisily; some men in the back row rushed outside to tell the people in the street.

The judge hammered on the bench. When the noise died down he addressed Mrs. Loo:

"Do you confess having murdered your husband by driving a nail into the top of his head?"

Mrs. Loo slowly raised her head. A long shiver shook her body.

199

Pushing a lock of hair away from her forehead, she said in a toneless voice:

"I confess."

A ripple of noise came from the audience as this final news also was relayed through the court hall. Judge Dee leaned back in his chair. When the hall was still again, he said in a tired voice:

"I shall now hear your confession."

Mrs. Loo drew her robe around her slight frame. She said forlornly:

"It seems so long ago now, does it really matter?" Leaning her back against the table, she looked up at the window high in the wall. Then she said suddenly:

"My husband, Loo Ming, was a dull, stupid man, what did he understand? How could I go on living with him, I, who was searching . . ." She heaved a deep sigh, then went on: "I had a daughter of him, then he said he wanted a son. I could not bear it any longer. One day he complained of a stomach ache, and I gave him strong wine as medicine, mixed with a sleeping powder. When he was sound asleep, I took the long nail I use for punching the holes in the soles of my shoes, and drove it with the mallet into the top of his skull, till only the head showed."

"Kill the witch!" someone shouted and angry exclamations followed. Quick to change their attitude, the fury of the crowd now directed itself against Mrs. Loo.

Judge Dee crashed on the bench with his gavel.

"Silence and order!" he shouted.

The hall was still at once. The authority of the tribunal had been restored.

"Dr. Kwang stated it was a heart attack," Mrs. Loo continued. She added contemptuously: "I had to be the mistress of that man in order to obtain his help. He thought he knew the secrets of magic, but he was only a useless beginner. As soon as he had signed the death certificate, I severed our relations. Then I was free . . .

"One day, about a month ago, I slipped in the snow when leaving my shop. A man helped me up, and led me inside. I sat on the bench in my shop, and he massaged my ankle. With every touch of his hand I felt the vital force with which this man vibrated. I knew that this was at last the partner I had been waiting for. I concentrated all my mental and physical powers to draw this man toward me, but I felt him resisting. Yet, when he left, I knew he would come back."

Something of her former animation came back to Mrs. Loo as she continued:

"And he came back! I had won. That man was as a burning flame. He loved and hated me at the same time, he hated himself for loving me, yet he loved me! It was the very roots of life that bound us together . . ."

She paused. Then she bent her head, and her voice was again tired as she went on:

"Then I knew that I was losing him again. He accused me of sapping his strength, of interfering with his disciplines. He told me we would have to part. . . . I was frantic, I could not live without that man, without him I felt the forces of life ebbing away from me. . . . I told him that if he left me, I would kill him just as I had killed my husband."

Shaking her head disconsolately she went on:

"I shouldn't have said that. I knew it by the look he gave me. All was over. Then I knew also that I had to kill him.

"I put the poison in a dried jasmine flower, and went to the

bathhouse dressed as a Tartar youth. I said I had come to offer
him my apologies, that I wanted to part from him on good terms.
He was coldly polite. When he didn't say anything about keeping
my secret, I dropped the flower in his teacup. As soon as the
poison took effect, he gave me one terrible look. He opened his
mouth but he could not speak. But I knew that he had cursed me,
and that I was lost. . . . Heaven, he was the only man I ever
loved . . . and I had to kill him."

Suddenly she raised her head. Looking straight at the judge
she said:

"Now I am dead. With my body you can do what you like!"

Judge Dee looked with horror at the sudden change that had
come over her. Deep lines had appeared on her smooth face, her
eyes had become dim, she had suddenly aged ten years. Now that
her indomitable, fierce spirit was gone, there was indeed nothing
left but an empty shell.

"Read out the confession!" he ordered the scribe.

Dead silence reigned in the hall while the scribe read out his
notes.

"Do you agree that this is your true confession?" the judge
asked.

Mrs. Loo nodded. The headman presented the document to her,
and she impressed her thumb mark on it.

Judge Dee closed the session.

Twenty-fourth Chapter: THE JUDGE GOES OUT ON A SECRET EXCURSION; HE PAYS A SECOND VISIT TO MEDICINE HILL

JUDGE DEE left the court hall, followed by his three lieutenants. There were some timid cheers from the crowd. As soon as they had entered the corridor, Ma Joong hit Chiao Tai with a resounding clap on his shoulder. They could hardly restrain their exultation. Even Tao Gan was chuckling happily as they entered Judge Dee's private office.

But when the judge turned around to them, they saw to their utter amazement that his face was as cold and impassive as during the session.

"It has been a long day," he said quietly. "Chiao Tai and Tao Gan had better go and take a rest. As for you, Ma Joong, I regret that I can't let you go yet."

When Chiao Tai and Tao Gan had left with a look of blank astonishment, Judge Dee took up his letter to the Prefect. He tore it up and threw the scraps on the glowing coals in the brazier. He

203

watched silently till they had turned to ash. Then he said to Ma Joong:

"Go and change into your hunting dress, Ma Joong. And have two horses stand ready in the courtyard."

Ma Joong was completely dumbfounded. He thought of asking for some explanation, but seeing the look on Judge Dee's face he silently went out.

In the courtyard the snow was falling in large flakes. Judge Dee looked up at the leaden sky.

"We'll have to hurry," he said to Ma Joong. "With this weather, it'll be dark soon."

He pulled his neckcloth up over the lower part of his face, and swung himself on his horse. They left the tribunal by the side gate.

Riding through the main street they saw that many people were crowding the street stalls despite the snow and the icy wind. Standing close together under the temporary roofs of oilcloth, they were eagerly discussing the sensational session of the tribunal. They paid no attention to the two horsemen riding past.

When they came to the north city gate, the cold blast from the plain hit them in the face. Judge Dee knocked on the door of the guardhouse with the handle of his whip. When a soldier appeared, he ordered him to hand Ma Joong a storm lantern of thick oil paper.

Outside the city the judge rode in a westerly direction. Dusk was falling now, but the snow seemed to grow less.

"Are we going far, Your Honor?" Ma Joong asked worriedly. "It's easy to get lost among the hills in this weather!"

"I know the way," Judge Dee replied curtly, "we'll soon be there."

He took the way leading to the cemetery.

When they had entered the graveyard the judge made his horse step slowly while he intently scrutinized the grave mounds. He went past the open grave of Loo Ming, and on to the farthest corner of the cemetery. There Judge Dee dismounted. With Ma Joong close on his heels, he wandered among the grave mounds, muttering to himself.

Suddenly the judge halted. With his sleeve he wiped the snow from the stone that closed a large mound. When he saw the name Wang chiseled in the slab, he said to Ma Joong:

"Here it is. Help me to open this grave; you'll find two short spades in my saddlebag."

Judge Dee and Ma Joong dug out the snow and earth accumulated along the base of the stone plate, then started to loosen it. It was a strenuous task, and when the slab finally could be made to topple forward, it had become dark. Heavy clouds obscured the moon.

The judge was perspiring despite the cold. He took the lighted lantern from Ma Joong, stooped and entered the tomb.

The stale air inside was curiously still. As Judge Dee lifted the lantern he saw that three coffins were standing in the vault. He scrutinized the inscriptions, then went to the end of the one on the right. "Hold the lantern!" he ordered Ma Joong, involuntarily lowering his voice.

Ma Joong looked anxiously at the face of the judge, haggard in the flickering light of the lantern. He saw him take a chisel from his sleeve. Using the spade as a hammer, he started to pry loose the lid. The blows resounded hollowly in the vault.

"Start on the other side!" he judge commanded.

Confused thoughts raced through Ma Joong's brain as he put the lantern on the floor and inserted his spade into the groove.

They were desecrating a grave. In this close space the air seemed nearly warm, but Ma Joong shivered violently.

He never knew how long they worked on the coffin. But his back was aching when at last they had loosened the lid. Using the spades as a lever they found they could lift it up.

"Let it drop down on the right!" Judge Dee panted.

They gave the lid a push, and it fell to the floor with a resounding crash.

The judge covered his mouth and nose with his neckcloth, and Ma Joong hastily followed his example.

The judge lifted the lantern over the open coffin. Inside lay a skeleton, the bones here and there still covered by the remains of the decayed shroud.

Ma Joong shrank back. Judge Dee gave him the lantern, then bent over the coffin and carefully felt the skull. When he saw it was loose, he took it out of the coffin and examined it closely. Ma Joong thought that in the uncertain light of the lantern the empty sockets of the skull seemed to leer at Judge Dee's face close by.

Suddenly the judge shook the skull. There was the sound of rattling metal. The judge peered at the top of the skull and felt it with the tip of his finger. Then he carefully replaced the skull in the coffin. He said hoarsely:

"That's all. Let's go back."

When they crept out of the vault they saw that the clouds had disappeared; a full moon was in the sky and cast its silvery rays over the deserted graveyard.

Judge Dee put the lantern out.

"Let's replace the stone slab," he said.

206

It took them a long time to get the stone back into its original position. Judge Dee shoveled the snow and mud back against the base, then mounted his horse.

When they were riding toward the gate of the cemetery, Ma Joong could no longer restrain his curiosity.

"Who was buried there, Your Honor?" he asked.

"You'll know tomorrow," Judge Dee replied. "During the morning session I shall initiate another murder investigation."

Arrived in front of the north city gate, the judge halted his horse. He said:

"After the snowstorm it has turned into a beautiful night now. You can go back to the tribunal, I shall take a ride through the hills to clear my mind."

Before Ma Joong could say anything the judge had turned his horse and was riding away.

He headed east. When he had come to the foot of the Medicine Hill, he halted. Bending over in his saddle he scrutinized the snow. Then he dismounted, fastened the reins to the tree stump, and began the ascent.

A slight figure clad in a gray fur cloak stood near the balustrade on top of the crag, looking out over the white plain below.

As she heard the sounds of Judge Dee's boots in the snow, she turned around slowly.

"I knew you would come here," she said quietly. "I was waiting for you."

When the judge remained standing silently in front of her, she went on quickly:

"Look, your robes are all dirty, and your boots are covered with mud! Have you been there?"

"Yes," Judge Dee answered slowly, "I went there, together with Ma Joong. That old murder must be investigated by the tribunal."

Her eyes grew wide. The judge looked past her, desperately seeking for words.

She drew the cloak close around her.

"I knew this would happen," she said in a toneless voice. "And yet . . ." She paused, then went on forlornly: "You don't know what . . ."

"I do know!" the judge interrupted her fiercely. "I know what made you act as you did five years ago, and I know that you . . . I know what made you tell me."

She bent her head and sobbed, strange, soundless sobs.

"The pattern must be restored," the judge continued in a broken voice, "even . . . if it destroys ourselves. Believe me, this is stronger than me myself. The days that come will be a living hell for you . . . and for me. I wish to Heaven I could do otherwise. But I can't. . . . And it was you who saved me! Forgive me . . . please!"

"Don't say that!" she cried out. Then, smiling through her tears, she added softly: "I knew, of course, what you would do, else I wouldn't have told you. I would never want you to be other than you are."

The judge wanted to speak but emotion strangled his voice. He gave her a despairing look.

She averted her eyes.

"Don't speak!" she panted. "And don't look at me. I can't bear to see . . ."

She buried her face in her hands. The judge stood motionless. He felt as if a cold sword were slowly cutting through his heart.

The last meeting on Medicine Hill

Suddenly she looked up. The judge wanted to speak, but she quickly laid her finger on her lips.

"Don't!" she said. Then she added with a tremulous smile: "Be still now! Don't you remember, about the blossoms falling down in the snow? If we listen, we can hear the sound . . ."

Gaily pointing at the tree behind him, she continued quickly: "Look, the blossoms came out today! Please, look!"

The judge turned around. As he lifted his head, the beauty of what he saw took his breath away. The tree stood silhouetted against the moonlit sky; the small red blossoms seemed like glittering red jewels covering the silvery boughs. A faint current stirred the cold air. A few petals detached themselves and slowly fluttered down on the snow below.

Suddenly he heard behind him the sound of splintering wood. He whirled around and saw the broken fence. He was alone on the crag.

Twenty-fifth Chapter: THE CORONER PROFFERS A STARTLING ACCUSATION; TWO OFFICIALS COME FROM THE IMPERIAL CAPITAL

THE next morning Judge Dee woke up late after a tormented night. The clerk who brought his morning tea said sadly:

"Our coroner's wife had an accident, Your Honor. Last night she went as usual to the Medicine Hill to gather herbs. She must have leaned over the balustrade and it gave away. At dawn a hunter found her dead body at the foot of the crag."

The judge expressed his regret, then ordered him to call Ma Joong. When they were alone the judge said gravely to him:

"Last night I made a mistake, Ma Joong. You must never tell anyone about our visit to the graveyard. Forget it!"

Ma Joong nodded his large head. He said quietly:

"I am not much use for brainwork, Your Honor, but the one thing I can do is follow orders. If Your Honor says 'Forget,' I forget."

Judge Dee dismissed him with an affectionate look.

A knock sounded on the door, and Kuo came in. The judge rose quickly and went to meet him. He formally expressed his condolences.

Kuo looked up at him with his large, sad eyes.

"It was no accident, Your Honor," he said calmly. "My wife knew that place like the palm of her hand, and the fence was quite strong. I know that she killed herself."

As Judge Dee raised his eyebrows, he continued in the same even voice:

"I confess being guilty of a serious crime, Your Honor. When I asked my wife to marry me, she warned me that she had killed her husband. I said it made no difference to me, because I knew her husband was a cruel brute who took delight in hurting men and animals alike. I feel that such persons ought to be destroyed, although I lack the courage to do it myself. I am not the kind of man who accomplishes great things, Your Honor."

He raised his hands in a hopeless gesture. Then he resumed:

"I did not ask her for particulars then, and the subject was never again mentioned between us. But I knew that she was often thinking about it, torn by doubts. I should of course have urged her to report the crime, but I am a selfish man, Your Honor. I could not bear the thought of losing her. . . ."

He stared at the floor, his mouth twitching.

"Then why do you raise this subject now?" Judge Dee asked.

Kuo looked up.

"Because I know it's her wish, Your Honor," he replied quietly. "I know that Mrs. Loo's trial affected her deeply; she felt she had to atone for her crime by killing herself. She was a woman of utter sincerity and I know she wishes her crime to be reported officially, so that she can enter the Hereafter with a clean record.

Therefore I come to report now, also accusing myself of being an accomplice after the deed."

"Do you realize that yours is a capital crime?" the judge asked.

"Of course!" Kuo said, amazed. "My wife knew that I wouldn't mind dying after she had passed away."

Judge Dee silently stroked his beard. He felt deeply shamed by this supreme loyalty. After a while he said:

"I cannot initiate a posthumous case against your wife, Kuo. She never told you how she killed her husband, and I cannot open a grave for an autopsy, just on hearsay evidence. Moreover, I think that if your wife really had intended that the crime she said she committed be reported, she would, of course, have left behind a written self-accusation."

"That is true," Kuo said pensively. "I hadn't thought of that. My mind is so confused. . . ." Then he added softly, as to himself: "It will be lonely. . . ."

Judge Dee left his chair and walked over to him. He asked:

"Isn't that small daughter of Mrs. Loo staying in your house?"

"Yes," Kuo said with a slow smile. "She's a nice little thing. My wife became very fond of her."

"Then your duty is clear, Kuo!" the judge said firmly. "As soon as the case against Mrs. Loo is closed, you will adopt the girl as your daughter."

Kuo gave the judge a grateful look. He said ruefully:

"I was so upset that I didn't even apologize for my failure to notice the nail during the first autopsy, Your Honor. I do hope . . ."

"Let's forget the past," Judge Dee interrupted quickly.

Kuo knelt and three times touched the floor with his forehead. When he had risen again he said simply:

"Thank you, sir." Turning to go he added: "Your Honor is a great and good man."

As Kuo slowly shuffled to the door, the judge felt as if he had been hit across the face with a heavy whip.

Staggering back to his desk he sat down heavily in his chair. Suddenly he thought of what Kuo had said about his wife's doubts. "Joy passes, it's remorse and sorrow that last"—she had indeed known the entire poem. "Oh that but once new love . . ." His head sank on the table.

After a long time he righted himself. A conversation with his father, long forgotten, suddenly came to his mind. Thirty years ago, when he had just passed his first literary examination, he had eagerly told his father his great plans for the future. "I trust you'll go far, Jen-djieh," his father had said, "but be prepared for much suffering on the way! And you'll find it very lonely—at the top." He had answered confidently: "Suffering and loneliness make a man strong, sir!" He had not understood his father's sad smile. But now he knew.

The clerk came in with a pot of hot tea, and the judge slowly drank a cup. Suddenly he thought, amazed: How strange that life goes on, as if nothing had happened. Yet Hoong died, a woman and a man made me deeply ashamed of myself, and I am sitting here, drinking my tea. Life goes on, but I have changed. It goes on, but I don't want to take part in it any longer.

He felt utterly tired. Peace, he thought, life in retirement. But then he knew he could not do it. Retirement was for men without obligations, but he had too many of those. He had sworn to serve the state and the people, he had married and begotten children. He could not be a defaulter, running like a coward away from his debts. He would go on.

Having taken this decision, the judge remained deep in thought.

Suddenly the door burst open, startling him from his reflections. His three lieutenants came running in.

"Your Honor!" Chiao Tai exclaimed excitedly, "two high officials have arrived from the capital! They traveled all through the night!"

Judge Dee gave them an astonished look. He told them to let the high-ranking visitors refresh themselves in the reception hall; he would present himself there as soon as he had put on his ceremonial robes.

When he entered the reception hall the judge saw two men clad in robes of shining brocade. He knew by the insignia on their caps that they were Senior Investigators of the Metropolitan Court of Justice. His heart sank as he knelt down. This must be a very serious matter.

The elder man quickly stepped up to him and raised the judge. He said respectfully:

"Your Excellency shall not kneel before his servants."

Dumbfounded, the judge let himself be led to the seat of honor.

The elder official went to the high altar table against the back wall, and carefully lifted up a yellow document roll that had been deposited there. Holding it reverently in both hands, he said:

"Your Excellency will now read the August Words."

Judge Dee rose, and with a bow accepted the document roll. He slowly unrolled it, taking care that the Imperial Seal he saw at the top was above the level of his eyes.

It was an Imperial Edict, stating in the customary formal phrases that Dee Jen-djieh, of Tai-yuan, in recognition of twelve years' meritorious service, had been appointed President of the Metropolitan Court. It bore the Emperor's fiat, written with the Vermilion Brush.

Judge Dee rolled up the Edict, and replaced it on the altar

215

Judge Dee reads an Imperial edict

table. Then, turning in the direction of the capital, he prostrated himself, and nine times knocked his forehead on the floor to express his gratitude for this Imperial favor.

As he rose the two officials bowed deeply before him.

"These two persons," the elder said respectfully, "have been appointed Your Excellency's assistants. We have taken the liberty of giving copies of the August Edict to the senior scribe, to be put up throughout the town, so that the people may rejoice in the honor bestowed upon their magistrate. Early tomorrow morning we shall escort Your Excellency to the capital. It is the August Will that Your Excellency be available for duty as soon as possible."

"Your Excellency's successor," the younger man added, "has already been appointed, and can be expected here tonight."

Judge Dee nodded.

"You may retire now," he said. "I shall proceed to my office to put the files in order for my successor."

"We shall give ourselves the honor of assisting Your Excellency," the elder man said obsequiously.

Walking back to the chancery the judge heard the sounds of firecrackers from afar. The citizens of Pei-chow had started to celebrate the success of their magistrate.

The senior scribe came to meet them. He announced that the personnel of the tribunal was waiting in the court hall to congratulate the judge.

When he ascended the dais, Judge Dee saw that all the scribes, clerks, constables and guards were kneeling in front of the bench, and this time his three lieutenants had joined them.

With the two Investigators standing on either side of him, the judge spoke a few appropriate words, thanking all for their service

217

during his term of office. He announced that all would receive a special bonus, in accordance with their rank and position. Then he looked at the three men who had so loyally served him, and had become his friends. He announced that Ma Joong and Chiao Tai were appointed Commanders of the Right and Left Wing of the Court Guards, and Tao Gan as General Secretary.

The acclamations of the personnel mingled with the loud cheers of the crowd that was assembling in the street outside. "Long live our magistrate!" they shouted. Judge Dee reflected bitterly what a comedy life really was.

When Judge Dee had gone back to his private office, Ma Joong, Chiao Tai and Tao Gan came rushing inside to thank him. But they abruptly halted in their steps when they saw the two solemn officials helping the judge to take off his ceremonial robes.

Over their heads the judge smiled bleakly at his lieutenants. They quickly withdrew. As the door closed behind them he realized with a sudden pang that the old days of easy comradeship were over.

The elder official presented to the judge his favorite fur bonnet. Reared in Court circles, he had learned to conceal his feelings. But he could not help raising one eyebrow as he looked at the old, worn fur.

"It is a rare honor," the younger official said suavely, "to be appointed directly to the exalted office of President. As a rule the August choice is made from among the elder Provincial Governors. And Your Excellency is only about fifty-five years old, I presume!"

Judge Dee reflected that the man was not very observant, he could have seen that he was barely forty-six. But as he looked in his mirror he saw to his utter amazement that during the past few days his black beard and whiskers had turned gray.

He sorted out the files on his desk, giving some brief explanations to the two officials. When he came to the file with his project for the farmer loans, on which he had worked so often with Sergeant Hoong, he could not help waxing enthusiastic. The two officials listened politely, but he soon perceived that they were plainly bored. With a sigh he closed the file. He remembered his father's words: "It's very lonely—at the top."

Judge Dee's three lieutenants were sitting in the guardhouse, around the log fire that was blazing in the middle of the stone floor. They had been talking about Sergeant Hoong; now they were looking silently into the flames.

Then Tao Gan said suddenly:

"I wonder whether I could interest those two panjandrums from the capital in a friendly little game of dice tonight!"

Ma Joong looked up.

"No more dice for you, Mister Secretary," he growled. "You'll have to learn to live up to your high status now. And Heaven be praised that now I'll be spared the dismal sight of that greasy caftan of yours."

"When we are in the capital I'll have it turned," Tao Gan replied placidly. "And no more vulgar fisticuffs for you, Ma Joong. Besides, isn't it time that you left the rough work to younger ones, eh, brother? I see gray hairs on your head, my friend."

Ma Joong felt his knees with his large hands.

"Well," he said ruefully, "I admit that I am getting a bit stiff in the limbs, now and then." Suddenly his face lit up in a broad grin. "But, brother, fine fellows like us will have the pick of the wenches in the capital!"

"Don't forget the competition of the young coxcombs in the capital," Tao Gan remarked dryly.

Ma Joong's face fell. He pensively scratched his head.

"Shut up, old sour-face!" Chiao Tai barked at Tao Gan. "Granted that we are getting on a bit in years and even enjoy a good night's rest sleeping alone, sometimes. But, brothers, there's one thing that'll never leave us!"

He raised his hand as if lifting a cup.

"The amber liquid!" Ma Joong shouted as he sprang up. "Come along, brothers, we'll go to the best place in town!"

Taking Tao Gan in their midst, they marched him off to the main gate.

POSTSCRIPT 1

THE case of the headless corpse is based on one related in a Chinese casebook of the thirteenth century, translated by me under the title *T'ang-yin pi-shih, Parallel Cases from under the Peartree, A thirteenth-century manual of jurisprudence and detection* (Sinica Leidensia Series, Vol. X, E. J. Brill, Leiden 1956). Case 64 of that handbook says that *c.* A.D. 950 a merchant found the headless corpse of his wife when he returned from a journey; the wife's family accused him of having murdered her, and he wrongly confessed under torture. A clever detective had doubts and started questioning all the undertakers of the district about unusual burials. One of them reported that he had buried for a wealthy man a dead maid, but that he had noticed that the coffin was extraordinarily light. The detective had it opened, and it was found to contain only a severed head. It then transpired that the wealthy man had killed the maid, and placed the headless body in the house of the absent merchant, whose wife he had taken as secret paramour. This meager story leaves much to the imagination and contains several improbabilities, such as the merchant's not seeing that the dead body was not that of his wife; these I tried to eliminate while working out the motif for the present novel.

The nail murder is one of the most famous motifs in Chinese crime literature. The oldest source is quoted in the casebook *T'ang-yin-pi-shih* mentioned above, in Case 16, where the solution is ascribed to Yen Tsun, a clever judge who lived in the beginning of our era. The point of these stories is always the same: the judge is baffled by the fact that although there are strong reasons for suspecting the wife, the body of the husband shows no signs of violence. The final discovery of the nail is elaborated in various ways. The oldest version says that Yen Tsun found it because he noticed that a swarm of flies congregated on one place on top of the dead man's skull. The latest version known to me occurs in the

221

eighteenth-century Chinese detective novel, *Wu-tse-t'ien-szu-ta-ch'i-an*, which I published in English translation under the title *Dee Goong An* (Tokyo 1949); there the judge finally elicits a confession from the guilty widow by staging in the tribunal a scene from hell which makes the woman think she is appearing before the Judge of the Nether World. Since this solution would not appeal to the Western reader, for the present novel I utilized quite another version, briefly recorded by G. C. Stent under the title *The Double Nail Murders,* and published in 1881 in Volume X of the *China Review.* When the coroner fails to discover any trace of violence on the victim's corpse, his own wife suggests to him that he look for a nail. When the judge has convicted the murdered man's widow on this evidence, he has also the coroner's wife brought before him, since her knowledge of such a subtle way of committing a murder seems suspicious to him. It transpires that the coroner is her second husband. The corpse of her first husband is exhumed, and a nail discovered inside the skull. Both women are executed.

In my preceding Judge Dee novels the magistrate always appears as the omnipotent, infallible judge who invariably gets the better of the criminals brought before him. In the present novel I tried to show the reverse of the medal, stressing the grave risks a magistrate incurred as soon as he made a mistake. It should be remembered that the magistrate's position of well-nigh absolute power and complete superiority over all persons brought before his bench was but borrowed glory, based not on his personal rank but derived solely from the prestige of the government he was temporarily appointed to represent. The law was inviolable, but not the judge who enacted it; magistrates could not claim for themselves immunity or any special privileges on the basis of their office. They were i.a. subject to the age-old Chinese legal principle of *fan-tso,* "reversed punishment," which implies that the person who wrongly accused another shall suffer the same punishment as the wronged person would have received if the accusation had been proved true. For this aspect of the case of Mrs. Loo, I utilized some traits described in *Dee Goong An.* At the same time I tried to comply with the—not unreasonable!—demand of some readers that the fair sex should play a greater role in Judge Dee's life.

As to my story of Yü Kang and Miss Liao, it should be noted that although the Chinese have always taken a very tolerant view concerning premarital sexual relations of a man, his future wife is strictly taboo. The reason is presumably that while relations with courtesans and unattached women are a man's private affair, his marriage was considered as affecting the entire family, including the ancestors, to whom this solemn act had to be reported with due ceremony. Consummation of the union before it had been officially announced to the ancestors was a grave insult to them, proving a criminal lack of piety. And since times immemorial the Chinese have classified impiety toward one's parents, whether dead or alive, in the legal category of *pu-tao*, "Impious crimes," which imply the death penalty in one of its more severe forms.

Ancestral worship is the cornerstone of Chinese religious life. Every family used to have its own household shrine containing the wooden tablets in which the spirits of the dead members of the family were supposed to dwell. The head of the house announced to these spirits important events in the family, and at regular times sacrifices of food were offered to them. Thus the dead continued to take part in the activities of the living, the unity of the family traversing the barrier between life and death. These facts explain the background of Chapter 21 of this novel.

Ancestral worship supplies also one of the reasons why the desecration of a grave was legally a capital offense. The Chinese Penal Code which was in force till the establishment of the Republic in 1911 states in Section CCLXXVI: "All persons guilty of digging in, and breaking up another man's burying ground, until at length one of the coffins which had been deposited therein, is bare and becomes visible, shall be punished with 100 blows, and perpetual banishment to the distance of 3,000 miles. Any person who, after having been guilty as aforesaid, proceeds to open the coffin, and uncover the corpse laid therein, shall be punished with death by being strangled, after undergoing the usual confinement" (cf. *Ta Tsing Leu Lee*, the Penal Code of China, translated from the Chinese by Sir George Thomas Staunton, London, 1810).

As regards the personality of the boxing master Lan Tao-kuei, it should be noted that Chinese boxing is a very old art, aimed at promoting one's own physical and mental health rather than at vanquishing an opponent. In the seventeenth century Chinese refugees introduced this art into Japan, where it was developed into the famous Japanese art of self-defense, *judo* or *jujitsu*. As to the relation between Master Lan and

Mrs. Loo I may remark that the ancient Chinese had certain theories which, if practiced in the left-handed way, resembled our medieval vampirism. Those interested will find more details in Dr. Joseph Needham's *Science and Civilisation in China* (Cambridge University Press, 1956), Vol. 2, page 146, where also my own publication on the subject is referred to.

The quarrel about the broken cakes and its solution used in Chapter 14 of the present novel is taken from the *T'ang-yin-pi-shih* mentioned above, Case 35. There its solution is ascribed to Sun Pao, a perspicacious judge of the beginning of our era.

The Seven Board, in Chinese called *Ch'i-chiao-pan*, "Seven Clever Board," or also *Chih-hui-pan*, "Wisdom Board," is an old Chinese invention that was especially popular during the sixteenth and seventeenth centuries. Then some well-known scholars published books with series of figures that can be made with the board. In the beginning of this century it found its way also to Western countries, and is still occasionally seen in toy shops.

Dr. R. H. van Gulik

224

It seemed superfluous to repeat here the description of ancient Chinese administration of justice printed in the Postscripts of the four previously published Judge Dee novels. Instead I add a few general remarks on those novels, thereby also supplying the answers to a few questions some readers addressed to me.

My interest in Chinese crime literature was aroused only after I had already been engaged for more than fifteen years in the study of Chinese language and history, namely when in 1940 I came upon an anonymous Chinese detective novel of the eighteenth century.* Since this book seemed to me of unusual interest, I prepared an English translation, which was publishd in 1949 in Tokyo under the title *Dee Goong An*. In my annotations I gave a list of books on Chinese crime literature and added: "It might be an interesting experiment if one of our modern writers of detective stories would try his hand at composing an ancient Chinese detective story himself. The pattern is given in the novel translated here, while in the books listed above one will find a rich variety of peculiarly Chinese plots" (page 231). When I noticed that the book market in China and Japan was flooded with bad translations of third-rate Western thrillers, I resolved to conduct the above-mentioned experiment myself, and mainly to prove to Oriental readers how rich their own ancient crime literature is in source material for modern detective stories. I had no previous experience in writing fiction, but I thought that if I relied heavily on my Chinese reading of past years and kept closely to the Chinese traditional pattern, it was worth trying. Thus in 1950 I wrote in

* I am proud to share the credit for having discovered the merits of old Chinese detective novels with so eminent an expert on crime literature as Vincent Starrett. That excellent storyteller became interested in the subject during his sojourn in China, and wrote the delightful essay "Some Chinese Detective Stories," found in his *Bookman's Holiday, the Private Satisfactions of an Incurable Collector,* published in 1942 by Random House, New York.

Tokyo *The Chinese Bell Murders,* and later that year *The Chinese Maze Murders.* Originally I had not intended to publish these two novels in English, my English manuscript was only a working draft to be used for a published version in Chinese and Japanese. Thereafter, when Western friends showed interest in this new type of detective novel, I had *The Chinese Maze Murders* published in English, as another experiment (first printed in 1956, in Holland; published in England). The success of that novel then led to the writing of three more, meant for both Oriental and Western readers. These were *The Chinese Lake Murders,* completed in 1952 in New Delhi; *The Chinese Nail Murders,* written in 1956 in Beirut, and *The Chinese Gold Murders,* written in 1958 in Beirut, in order to provide the series with a suitable opening volume. Although the five novels were written in the order mentioned, in the Judge Dee chronology—which is of course wholly fictitious—the right sequence in which they should be read is Gold-Lake-Bell-Maze-Nail Murders.

Although the actual writing of each novel was completed in six weeks or so, the preliminary work took considerably longer. Yet the laying of the groundwork afforded me as much pleasure as the writing itself, especially since this task could be performed piecemeal, as a welcome relaxation in between often exacting official duties. First I had to locate in old Chinese sources some plots suitable for being woven together into one longer novel about Judge Dee. Sometimes I found a plot complete in all details in ancient Chinese crime literature, at other times the main idea was suggested by only a few lines in a criminological or medical book, or by a brief anecdote in some other book or essay. In *The Chinese Bell Murders* all three plots are derived from Chinese sources, but in the four other novels I myself had to supply a considerable part of the intrigue, as will come to light if one consults the references to the sources listed in the Postscripts.

I chose Judge Dee as the central figure because we know much more about him than about other famous master detectives of China's past. The historical records are especially explicit on Judge Dee's career at the Imperial Court, and the detailed description of his achievements in that second phase of his life enables us to form a clearly delineated picture of the kind of man he was. He figures largely in Lin Yutang's recent historical novel, *Lady Wu, a True Story* (London 1959), where he is called "the greatest man of his generation." I here reproduce a portrait of "Judge Dee" when he was about 68 years old, wearing the full Court dress of a Minister of State; in his right hand he carries an ivory tablet, symbol of his rank. The portrait is taken from the block-print entitled *Ku-chin-sheng-hsien-t'u-k'ao*, a collection of pictures of famous people, published in 1830 by the scholar Ku Yüan, who utilized portraits in ancestral temples and similar ancient material.

As regards his four lieutenants, Sergeant Hoong, Ma Joong, Chiao Tai and Tao Gan, I adopted the names and main characteristics of this— entirely fictitious—quartet as I found them ready-made in the novel *Dee Goong An* mentioned above, but I elaborated their personalities according to my own fancy. For the other persons to be assigned a part in my stories I could pick and choose from the nearly unlimited variety of types described in Chinese historical records, and old novels and short stories.

After the plots and the persons concerned in them had been chosen, I had then to create a suitable geographical background. The place of action of each novel had to be a town-district somewhere in China and in particular the tribunal of that town, in old Chinese novels invariably the scene of all more important developments. I order to reduce the unavoidable repetition to a minimum, I purposely made each novel deal with Judge Dee's first few months on a new post. That gave me occasion to create each time an entirely different milieu as background.

Before elaborating this background, I first drew a sketch map of an imaginary town, an engaging task that often suggested new ideas for further developing the plot. Every old Chinese town had approximately the same landmarks: in the first place, of course, the tribunal, then the Temple of Confucius, the Temple of the War God, the Drum Tower, etc. The rest of the city one can design according to one's fancy, incorporating special features of towns actually visited or lived in. These maps, drawn in the traditional Chinese semipictorial manner, are found on the endpapers of each novel.

The last phase of the preliminary work was to draw up a timetable, divided in as many days as the action occupies, and each day subdivided into morning, afternoon and evening. In the novels there is little mention of dates and hours, because the ancient Chinese did not live by the clock as modern life compels us to do. But I needed a timetable for my own reference, so as to know where all my people were at a given moment, and what mischief they were up to there.

227

All this preliminary work having been completed, I could at last start to write. With plots, persons and places ready, the actual writing proceeded comparatively smoothly, all kinds of odds and ends coming to mind and finding their appropriate place. An apt retort quoted in an old novel, a joke exchanged between ricksha coolies, a striking pronouncement in a philosophical text, scraps of conversation overheard in a tea house—all such tidbits came as grist to my mill. The greatest difficulty was to prevent my characters from getting out of hand. I often became so engrossed in a certain character that I was tempted to let him or her engage in all kinds of activities that had no direct or indirect bearing on the plot—and such are out of place in a detective novel.

The characterization of Judge Dee presented one difficulty, namely that according to the time-honored Chinese tradition the detective may not show any human weaknesses, and never allow himself to become emotionally involved in the cases he deals with. Since personally I have little use for the completely aloof, superhuman detective, I tried to reach for Judge Dee a compromise between the "superman" dictated by Chinese tradition, and a more human type of person preferred by me—and probably by many readers, too. I tried to achieve this compromise by stressing those traits in Judge Dee which are felt by us as shortcomings, while the old-fashioned Chinese reader, on the contrary, takes those same traits for granted, or even considers them as virtues. I mention, for instance, Judge Dee's ultra-Confucianist mental attitude, including a narrow-minded view of poetry and painting; his unshakable conviction that everything Chinese is *ipso facto* superior, and his consequent disdain for the "foreign barbarians"; his prejudice against Buddhism and Taoism, although those are much more elevated in thought than Confucianism, which is in fact a rule of conduct rather than a religion; etc. Further, Judge Dee's taking for granted that filial piety implies that daughters meekly let their parents sell them as prostitutes; his condoning torture, and the general maltreatment of men and women before his bench, and his conforming without protest to the laws that prescribe various methods of capital punishment of inhuman cruelty. Stressing these and like points helped to present Judge Dee as a real person. Glossing them over would have been tantamount to falsifying the historical picture, for in ancient China even high-minded and progressive men had ethical standards in many respects different from ours. Yet we should be careful in passing judgment on cruder manners and morals of other times. When I consider the remarkable achievements of modern man in wholesale torture and murder in concentration camps, and especially in mass destruction of human life as made possible by the latest progress in mechanical warfare, I cannot help thinking that most of the cruelties committed in former ages were only the clumsy efforts of rank amateurs.

When the novel had been written, there still remained the task of devising an introductory episode covertly indicating the story's main events. I retained this interesting feature of most old Chinese novels, chiefly because it supplied me with a convenient means for introducing the reader to the Chinese atmosphere; for there will not be many readers who after having finished the novel have time and inclination for re-reading the beginning. The device was invented for the delectation of the Chinese reader of a former age, who considered all haste as a funda-mental error, and was wont to read and reread his novels from beginning to end, tracing the plot in every detail. It may be added that these intro-ductory episodes are supposed to have happened in the Ming dynasty, say *circa* A.D. 1600; that is to say about three hundred and fifty years ago, and about nine hundred years after Judge Dee's time. I also retained the Chinese custom of placing an edifying poem at the beginning of the book, and also the chapter headings in two more or less parallel lines.

Although I generally followed in my novels the old Chinese tradition, I deviated from it in two important points. First, in my novels the criminal's identity is revealed only at the end. Old Chinese crime stories, on the contrary, betray this important secret at the beginning; the subsequent detailed description of the moves and countermoves of detective and criminal provided the sedate Chinese reader with an enjoy-ment comparable to that derived from watching a game of chess. I thought that in this respect I had to make a concession to the modern Oriental and Western reader. Second, I kept the number of *dramatis personae* limited to about two dozen. Old Chinese novels as a rule have a cast at least ten times that size. This does not bother the Chinese reader, who has a prodigious memory for names and a sixth sense for family relationships, and who therefore likes his novels to be generously popu-lated. Since one cannot expect the same from the modern Western reader, in my novels I kept to casts of a more modest size and, more-over, spelled their names in such a manner as to be fairly easily remembered. Some readers, however, have remarked that even these limited casts are too large. In the new series of Judge Dee novels I am now preparing I therefore use a cast of only about twelve.

It was my aim to acquaint the reader with all the clues Judge Dee and his assistants discover, so that a—largely hypothetical!—reader who would study the novel line by line with a pad and pencil at hand, would be able to work out for himself the final solution. At the same time I thought it my good right to gloss over those clues by the various approved means.

As regards the style of my novels, I followed the Chinese tradition that a novel must be written in a simple, factual prose, and that descriptive passages must be limited to the absolute minimum. Chinese novelists concentrated on exciting action and deft dialogue, always remembering the main rule governing all forms of Chinese literary expression: "Say much in few words." Thus also in the matter of style I am greatly indebted to my Chinese predecessors in crime fiction.

Finally, I may say a few words about a delicate subject, namely the supernatural element. In old Chinese crime literature ghosts and goblins roam freely about, dogs, cats, spiders, monkeys and even kitchen utensils prove to possess the faculty of speech and deliver testimony in court. Such traits are, of course, incompatible with the modern principle that a detective novel should be as realistic as possible. However, I thought that a discreet use of this traditional Chinese element would not offend the reader, including those who hold more decided views on these matters than I. Since we of the present know little more about supernatural phenomena than did Judge Dee twelve hundred years ago, I prefer to sum up here the main supernatural traits of my five novels in the form of open questions, leaving it to the reader to decide what actually happened.

Did the sanctimonious collector of Sung celadon who narrates the opening episode of *The Chinese Bell Murders* really see in the old mirror all those frightful happenings? Or had he been sickening for a malicious fever that reached a crisis during his visit to the curio shop? In the latter case it is only natural that his interest in Judge Dee, and his affection for his two concubines (Apricot and Blue Jade of the novel), figured largely in his subsequent delirious visions.

Did the student of crime literature who appears in the opening episode of *The Chinese Maze Murders* really meet a descendant of Judge Dee in the restaurant on the Lotus Pond, or did he only have there a dream wherein the persons he had seen passing by occupied an important place? And did Master Crane Robe in Chapter XIX of that same novel possess esoteric knowledge, or were the clues Judge Dee obtained in his abode only the logical consequence of the Master's close association with the dead Governor?

The depraved Inspector who is introduced in the first pages of *The Chinese Lake Murders* was through an emotional conflict in such an unbalanced state of mind that he even contemplated suicide. Did his finding the dead body of a beautiful woman—who for some reason or other had drowned herself—bring him under the delusion that she was alive and told him the details of his own nefarious plot? Or was it the vengeful ghost of Almond Blossom who took possession of the corpse and thereafter haunted her victim till he died, broken in mind and body?

Did the old scribe appearing in *The Chinese Gold Murders* really change on occasion into a were-tiger? In that case it was he who was seen in the forest by Judge Dee and his two hefty lieutenants. If, on the other hand, the reader refuses to admit the existence of were-animals, then Judge Dee saw a real tiger, which had a white spot on its paw that caused it to be mistaken for a white, human hand. And in that case the old scribe's confession can be dismissed as the vagaries of an old man's diseased mind. As to the ghostly apparitions mentioned in that novel, those find in the end their perfectly natural explanation—all except one, that is!

Finally, the henpecked husband who relates the opening passage of the present novel, *The Chinese Nail Murders,* had that evening been engrossed in his research on Judge Dee, and he had directly thereafter written a long letter to his beloved brother. Did he really meet the latter's ghost in his garden pavilion? Or was it but a dream, whereto Judge Dee, his brother and his own argumentative First Lady (Mrs. Loo of the novel) each contributed their share?

All these puzzles end up with the very same question mark as do most personal problems we are confronted with by this perplexing life of ours. And probably this was so disposed for our good.

Dr. R. H. van Gulik

THE JUDGE DEE DETECTIVE SERIES

THE CHINESE BELL MURDERS: *A Judge Dee Detective Story*
ISBN 0-06-072888-4 (paperback)
With this book, originally published in 1958, Van Gulik
introduces seventh-century super-sleuth Judge Dee as he
unravels the murder of a young girl, grapples with a clan of
homicidal monks, and resolves a longstanding feud between
the city's most important families.

THE CHINESE GOLD MURDERS
A Judge Dee Detective Story
ISBN 0-06-072867-1 (paperback)
Judge Dee has just been appointed magistrate of Peng-lai—
a desolate northeast Chinese village that appears harmless
but is in fact brimming with murder and intrigue. There
he battles army deserters, solves the mystery of his
predecessor's murder, and brings the killer to justice.

THE CHINESE LAKE MURDERS: *A Judge Dee Detective Story*
ISBN 0-06-075140-1 (paperback)
Dee has been sent to the city of Han-yuan to investigate the
embezzlement of government funds. But this case proves to be
only the first in a series of challenging mysteries. And amidst
it all, Dee must contend with the machinations of a dangerous
sect called the White Lotus.

THE CHINESE NAIL MURDERS
A Judge Dee Detective Story
ISBN 0-06-075139-8 (paperback)
Judge Dee has been appointed magistrate of Pei-chow,
a distant frontier district in China's barren north,
where he is faced with a fiendish murder involving
the nude, headless body of a woman, the disapparence
of a girl in love, and the stealing of precious jewels.

Don't miss the next book by your favorite author.
Sign up for AuthorTracker by visiting *www.AuthorTracker.com*.

Available wherever books are sold, or call 1-800-331-3761 to order.